THE RELUCTANT UBER GURU

He started driving for money. He kept driving for meaning.

A Contemporary Fable

by

DIANE DEMETRE

CHAPTER ONE

I N ALL HIS YEARS, NICK Stavros had never known such pain, not just in his body, but in the very essence of his being. Every cell seemed to weep in sorrow, using the whole of him as their wailing wall. His head throbbed with a primal pounding, as if a wild beast had been caged within his skull, desperate to escape. His skin burned with shame; a hellish fire lit by the match of his own remorse. But it was his heart that betrayed him most. Each beat, too fast, too loud, too unforgiving, thundered through his chest like a judge's gavel, delivering sentence after sentence of guilt. Sometimes, it felt as though it might rupture from the weight of it all, spilling his life force into the hollow cavern he had become. And how he wished it would. What mercy that would be. What blessed, beautiful release.

Eventually, they would find him—another morsel of news to fill a thirty-second slot on local MSM. *A seventy-year-old man was found dead in a car at Airlie Beach. Cause of death: heart failure. No suspicious circumstances.* His devoted wife would bury him in the cemetery plot he'd purchased a few years earlier, surrounded by his children and a few friends. Clean and convenient. Tidy, like the way he used to file boardroom papers and brush aside inconvenient truths.

None of them would be the wiser. None would know what a complete and utter arsehole he'd been. But Nick knew. He knew it in the marrow of his bones, in the sickened churn of his gut, in the echoing hollowness of a life unravelled. And he knew he wouldn't be that lucky, not anymore. He'd been lucky once. Lucky in business. Lucky in love. Lucky that the lies he told himself passed for truths—for a time.

But luck had a way of running out. And when it did, it left a bad taste in your mouth.

He'd fucked everything up and hadn't the faintest clue how to fix it. The mess he'd made wasn't something you could apologise away or sweep under the plush carpet of a well-appointed home. It was too big, too deep. And now, here he was, an old man marooned in his own failure, stranded between the man he'd been and the man he couldn't quite find.

A couple of weeks earlier, he'd driven to a nearby hang-gliding location, planning to drive off the edge of the mountain—a quick, clean exit. Nothing drawn out. No pills, no drama. Just one final acceleration into silence. But being the coward he knew himself to be, he just sat there, engine idling, hands on the wheel. Hoping. Wishing. Praying that the hand of God, or fate, or something beyond the puny power of his own will, would reach down and end it for him.

Yet here he was. Still breathing. Still broken. Same misery, different backdrop.

It seemed God wasn't in the business of mercy killings. Not for the likes of him.

He blinked against the glare as his gaze drifted across the ocean's palette of blues; deep indigo folding into cobalt, melting into turquoise, washing against the shore like a slow, rhythmic lullaby. And in that rarest of moments, his chest loosened. A breath, unbidden and unhurried, escaped his lips.

For a fleeting second, it was as if life pressed pause. The torment dulled; the ache softened. Just Nick and the sea. And with that, his thoughts backtracked, slowly and reluctantly, like a man retracing the steps of a crime scene he'd tried to forget.

Five years ago, he was riding high, living the good life with the wind at his back and the future paved in gold. Over decades of relentless hustle, he'd carved a small empire from sheer grit and savvy. He and Michele, his wife, his partner in every sense of the word, had built a thriving international business from scratch. Together, they'd stacked their dreams one brick at a time until they were standing on top of the world, toasting their success with French champagne in luxury resorts scattered across the globe.

They had it all: a stunning waterfront home, sun-drenched holidays overseas, a close-knit circle of friends, and a rock-solid marriage that had weathered twenty-plus years of life's squalls. The ultimate power couple: work hard, play hard, love fiercely. Their marriage was more than a union. It was an alliance, a dance of equals who had conquered the business world and were poised to ease into a self-funded retirement with nothing but time and pleasure ahead.

Then the world flipped on its axis. The pandemic struck like a thief in the night, not just stealing livelihoods but rewriting the rules of reality. To Nick, it was a con, an orchestrated globalist farce riddled with half-truths and power grabs. Under the crushing weight of government overreach, their business, once a monument to success, was shuttered. Permanently. Hundreds of their staff lost their jobs, and they lost everything. Not because of poor choices or bad management, but because truth had become the first casualty in a world gone mad.

Since that day, the man who had once walked tall with charm and confidence had been reduced to a shell. Nick Stavros, the charismatic leader with the golden touch, began slipping through the cracks of his own identity.

He spiralled, passing through the stages of grief like a ghost chasing something already lost. Denial clung to him in those early days, whispering that things would bounce back. That the world would right itself. That sanity would return. But within months, he realised just how naïve that hope had been.

In its place came rage—seething, acidic, and unrelenting. He became unbearable. A snarling, sarcastic bully with a temper that scorched everyone in its path, online or off. He haunted social media like a man possessed, feeding on fury, joining digital mobs as they tore down the idiocy of woke culture and the bureaucracy strangling the country's soul. The world had tipped into madness, and he roared into the void, powerless to stop it.

Then came the bargaining. The desperate prayers. Deals with a silent God. Promises whispered into the night, but there was no reply. No sign. No grace. Only the slow descent into despair.

Michele had tried. God, she had tried. She begged him to get help. Held him when he couldn't hold himself. Pleaded with him to reach for something, anything, before he slipped too far. But Nick had turned away, too proud, too stubborn, too lost.

And now, on this glorious autumn day, with the sunlight kissing the waves in playful glints, he sat in the deepest darkness he'd ever known.

"What a fucking loser," he said, his voice rough with self-loathing, catching sight of himself in the rear-view mirror. He couldn't hold the gaze. He yanked the mirror aside, turning away from the wreckage staring back at him.

He dropped his head onto the steering wheel, arms folded, eyes screwed shut. He wanted to cry, but the tears wouldn't come. Couldn't come. Good Greek boys didn't cry. They bore it. Swallowed it. Took it on the chin.

Be strong. Be a man.

"And how's that working out for you?" he muttered.

"Fuck. Fuck. Fuck!" Each word was punctuated by a pounding fist on the steering wheel. "I've got to tell her. I can't keep doing this. I can't keep lying."

With a shaky breath, he shoved the key into the ignition, dragged the car into reverse, and spun out of the car park. Gravel scattered behind him like the debris of his crumbling facade. It would take hours to get home. But maybe, just maybe, that was enough time to figure out how to break the worst news of his life to the woman he still loved more than anything.

* * *

STANDING AT THE sliding patio door in the bedroom, Michele gazed out at the magnificent view of the Pacific Ocean. Her arms wrapped around her body, the only embrace she could rely on these days. The kind of hug she used to receive from Nick—solid, safe, threaded with meaning. But now he was little more than a ghost walking through their home. A silent phantom. A man-shaped absence she could no longer reach.

For months, she'd been holding herself together with the same arms that once held him. And every day, like this one, she found herself here, scanning the horizon, hoping the ocean might give her answers the silence would not.

No matter how softly she asked, how bitterly she cried, how fiercely she demanded, Nick remained unreachable. He didn't meet her halfway. He didn't meet her at all. Conversations had turned to monologues, warmth to frost, closeness to aching distance. Their marriage, once so full of laughter and late-night whispers, was now unravelling thread by thread, and she was powerless to weave it back together.

She'd spent months combing through the past like an investigator at a cold crime scene. Replaying words. Reconstructing glances. Looking for clues. The more he pulled away, the more desperately she reached. But every time she tried to close the gap, it widened. He offered her nothing but silence, and in its place, she hurled accusations, cross-examining him, poking at the wounds, trying to provoke anything. Even anger would have been better than his cold, empty stare.

Something was wrong. Deeply wrong. And though her gut whispered the truth in fragments, she needed more than intuition. She needed confirmation. She needed something she could hold in her hands and say: *Yes, this is real. This is why he's slipping away.*

Even her meditations had failed her. The still, small voice within, the one she had trusted for decades, had gone silent. Not absent. Just unreachable, muffled by the static of her own suffering. She, who had taught others to go within and find stillness, now found only storm. She who had danced with divine timing and trusted synchronicity now stood deaf at the door of her own inner sanctuary.

She knew why. She wasn't blind to her own inner workings. Her desperation had created a wall. And until she could find her centre again, her guidance would remain elusive, just beyond reach. Still, she whispered to the ocean, the one constant in her life that never turned its back: "Where is he?" Her voice barely stirred the air.

But the question reached further than yesterday's unanswered departure. It wasn't just about his absence from the house. It was about his absence from everything. From them. From himself. Where had her once-loving, magnetic husband gone?

The man who used to light up a room with his presence, whose laughter came easily, and whose hands knew just how to find hers in the dark. The man who held her dreams with care, who'd once looked at her like she was his home. That man was nowhere to be found. In his place stood a stranger cloaked in shadows, trapped behind a wall she couldn't scale. It was as if he were being held captive by some dark villain she couldn't name, let alone negotiate with. A force that spoke in silence, that drained the light from his eyes and left only exhaustion and emptiness in its wake. No ransom note. No trail to follow. Just a slow, agonizing vanishing act.

She had tried everything. Words. Tears. Anger. Stillness. Prayer. Nothing broke the spell. Nothing brought him back. What haunted her most wasn't that he had changed. It was that he hadn't fought it. He'd surrendered. As if some part of him had already decided he wasn't worth rescuing.

Though she knew better than to fight shadows with force, she didn't know how to surrender either. Not like this. Not without a sign. Not without knowing whether there was still something left to save. Her eyes scanned the horizon, hoping for a glimmer. A shift in the tide. Anything. But the ocean, like Nick, remained mute.

As she did so often lately, Michele's gaze drifted toward the cluster of photo frames beside the bed. They sat like little sentinels on the dresser, silent witnesses to a life that once pulsed with adventure, passion, and purpose.

She reached for one without thinking—their wedding day. Nick's face beamed with besotted devotion, his eyes drinking her in like she was the answer to every prayer he'd ever whispered. In the image, they were mid-step, walking back down the aisle as husband and wife, smiles so wide they looked almost foolish with joy. He had adored her then. And she had loved him with the kind of fire people spend lifetimes chasing. Other frames joined the chorus. Their windswept silhouettes standing triumphantly atop snow-capped peaks. The sun-kissed glow of Mediterranean evenings, cocktails in hand, laughter spilling into the sea air. Moments frozen in time, unapologetically happy, radiating the gratitude they both had for the life they'd built from grit and love.

They weren't just memories. They were proof. Proof of who they'd been, of the bond they once believed was unbreakable. Of what they could be again… if only.

A soft smile curled her lips, a faint blush of warmth flickering beneath the ache. She could still see it, feel it— the way they first met. That slow-burn magnetism, the instant pull. Their steamy love affair, the kind that scorched the rule book and left no room for doubt. A love that most only dreamed of. And yet, despite the clarity with which she remembered it, the excitement had long since disappeared.

She was past crying; past the sharp edges of grief. There were no tears left—only the dull throb of fear gnawing at the edges of her heart like a rodent in the walls. It whispered things she didn't want to hear. Things she tried to silence. But fear had moved in now, quietly, persistently, leading her toward paths she never imagined she'd tread.

She had given her all. When they first met, she'd walked away from her own dream of moving and working overseas. She sacrificed it without resentment because of being with Nick, building something meaningful, and becoming a stepmother to his children. It had felt like the higher path. They'd become partners in everything—business, life, even the cause. Side by side, they'd stood firm against the propaganda of the Covid Cult. Together, they had spoken truth when truth was unfashionable, called out the cowardice of compliance, and held strong as their business was dismantled by the blind idiocy of government mandates. Yet, when the dust settled, it was clear Nick hadn't landed on his feet. She had pivoted, rebuilt, recalibrated. He hadn't. He couldn't.

She'd reminded him, gently at first, then more firmly, "You can't control what happens to you, but you can control how you respond to it." But her pragmatic wisdom only seemed to infuriate him. Truth was a mirror into which he didn't want to look. Especially when it came from her. It was as if her strength only reminded him of his weakness.

The ocean called her gaze once more, a merciful interruption from the swirling vortex of self-doubt and sorrow. It shimmered under the afternoon light, a vast and patient presence. Steady. Eternal. She pressed both palms to her chest, her fingertips resting over the tender pulse of her heart.

"What would you have me do? What would you have me say?" Her voice, no louder than a whisper, carried the weight of a soul seeking refuge. Michele's eyes glistened, though she couldn't be sure if it was the glare off the water or the single tear trying to form; one last lonely tear that hadn't yet given up the fight.

The rattle of the garage door cracked through the stillness, snapping her out of the spiral. Nick was home. A thousand feelings surged at once: relief, dread, hope, fatigue. But habit was quicker than thought. She straightened, turned, and hurried into the bathroom. In the mirror, she barely recognised the woman staring back at her—graceful, yes, but hollowed out around the edges. Still, she applied a swipe of lipstick, dabbed her cheeks with blush, and forced a smile to rise from somewhere deep within. The same ritual she'd performed countless times over the past year. Paint on the face. Brace the heart.

Again, she would try.

Again, she would reach out.

Again, she would play the good wife, the patient wife, the hopeful wife, the resilient wife.

"Turn the other cheek."

The words floated up from her childhood, a well-worn teaching from those distant Sunday School days. One of Jesus's gentler commands. Not weakness, but willingness. Not silence, but strength wrapped in mercy.

Yes… she would turn the other cheek. Not because she was a martyr. Not because she was naive. But because something inside her still believed in the man behind the silence. She still believed in the bond they once shared, and still believed that grace could be a beginning.

Again, she would choose to stand open.

Again, she would be willing to start over.

Again.

CHAPTER TWO

COMING HOME HAD BECOME BITTERSWEET. For Nick, the driveway was now a gauntlet of shame. Not just because of the ghost of his broken marriage lingering in every windowpane, but because of that gaping space in the garage where his beloved Corvette used to live. Now, it stood empty—like him. He cut the engine and sat for a moment, staring at the void. A lonely Corvette flag hung above where the car once parked, a final reminder of what once was. Another thing gone. Another piece of him stripped away. Bad investments. Bad timing. Bad decisions. One by one, they'd come knocking, and he'd paid the price.

His eyes slid up to the rear-view mirror, locking onto his own reflection. "You fucking idiot," he muttered.

The man staring back wasn't the one who used to run an international business empire. This one looked tired. Older. Beaten. He still couldn't wrap his head around it all, how their life had crumbled so fast. Losing the business to the circus that was Covid and watching his carefully cultivated investment portfolio burn to ashes was incomprehensible. His financial harvest, built over decades, had withered in just a few years. Everything he'd worked for, gone. And every time he came home, the missing Corvette screamed it at him again: *Failure. Inadequate. Not a man.*

"Forget all that shit," he growled, grabbing the bunch of red roses from the passenger seat. He glanced down at them, lip curling in self-disgust. *A dozen roses to fix the wreckage of my own making. Nice try, Romeo.*

Still, he climbed out, jaw clenched. As he crossed the threshold, the house greeted him not with warmth but with the stale tension of a marriage that had gone too long without a resolution. It used to be his sanctuary. Now it felt more like a cell.

"Nick. You're back." Michele's voice floated down the hallway, light, but tight at the edges. It was the same voice she used when she was trying. And she was always trying—more than he deserved.

He stepped into the kitchen, attempting to muster a smile. Michele stood by the sink, radiant even in her sadness. She wore that brave smile, the one he'd seen far too often lately. The one that broke his heart.

She turned toward him, her expression softening when she saw the roses.

"They're for you," he said, holding them out like a kid caught red-handed. "I do love you." He tried to sound sincere, but it came out awkward. Thin.

"Thank you, darling." She took the flowers gently, brushing her fingers against his. "I'll pop these in a vase."

She turned, moving with practiced grace, her tone casual as she asked, "So… how did your trip go? Where did you end up?"

Nick shifted on his feet. "I just needed to clear my head. I drove… I don't know… ended up at Airlie Beach."

She glanced over her shoulder, arranging the roses. "That's a long drive."

"Yeah."

"Did it help? Are you feeling better?"

Nick hesitated. A million thoughts stormed through his head, but he couldn't seem to lasso one. "Maybe. A little."

Pathetic. Tell her the truth. You said you would.

But the words caught in his throat. She was talking again, about her day, something she'd seen online, a podcast she'd heard, but he could barely hear her over the war inside his own head.

Then she said it. "So… what have you decided?"

The question yanked him back into the moment. "What do you mean?" he asked, already on the defensive.

"Well, what are you going to do?" She turned to face him. "Everyone needs a purpose. I know things haven't worked out the way you wanted, but it's time to move on, darling. Find something that gives your life meaning."

She's right. Of course, she's right.

But her words hit like a slap, slicing through his fragile calm.

"I've just walked in, and you start again." His voice was sharper than he intended, laced with accusation and guilt.

Her face fell. Just slightly. But it was enough.

He hated himself in that moment. Hated how he twisted her kindness into an attack. She was trying to pull him from the abyss, and he was the one pushing her away.

Unable to face her, he turned on his heel and stormed down the hallway.

Arsehole.

Coward.

You said you'd tell her. You said you'd stop hiding.

He strode to the bar in the summer house, poured himself a scotch, chugged a burning swallow, then lit a cigarette with shaking hands. His sanctuary now reeked of avoidance. Michele wouldn't follow. She never did. Not because she didn't care, but because she knew when he needed space.

He stood, staring at nothing. The smoke curled upward, and with it, his resolve disintegrated. He hated who he'd become. The lies. The distance. The coldness. He hated how he treated her. He hated that he had become the villain in the love story they once shared. And yet, beneath all that hate, one word still echoed.

Purpose.

She was right. He'd lost his way and lost his reason for waking up. Making money, running businesses, being the provider—that had always given him structure, identity, and worth. He'd been good at it. More than good. He'd excelled. But now? Now, he had nothing to offer. Now, he stood stewing in failure, looking for meaning in the bottom of a glass.

Find a purpose.

God, he wanted to. But for the life of him, he couldn't see it. He wasn't searching for purpose anymore. He was searching for comfort and relief. And in his lowest moments, he'd gone looking for it in all the wrong places. He lit another cigarette, the flick of the lighter breaking the silence like a cough in a confessional. The first inhale was always the worst, bitter and acrid, but the ritual gave his hands something to do, gave his mind a momentary distraction. As the smoke curled around him like a shroud, he drifted back to where it all began.

He'd been just a boy, barely tall enough to climb onto his grandfather's lap, but it was always his favourite place in the world. His Papou, blind but never bitter, had the kind of presence that didn't need sight to see straight into your soul. Nick could still feel the texture of the old man's trousers beneath his small legs, the scratch of wool softened only by years of wear. Papou had smelled of tobacco and ouzo, a scent that wrapped around Nick like a second skin every time he clambered into his lap. And even though he couldn't see, Papou always seemed to know exactly what Nick needed to hear.

As the adults laughed and gossiped around them at noisy family gatherings, Papou would puff steadily on his cigarettes that young Nick would light for him. One after the other, he'd share wisdom carved from a life, hard-lived but deeply loved.

"Respect your parents, my boy. Be kind. Work hard. Help others, especially those who can't help themselves."

Nick had nodded, solemn and wide-eyed, not yet realising how sacred those words would become.

His Papou's voice had dipped lower, almost conspiratorial. *"And above all, place love, loyalty, and legacy before anything else. That's how you live a good life, Nikos."*

Nick remembered the moment Papou blew out a thick ring of smoke, his yellow-stained fingers catching the light as he lifted them with reverence, like a priest offering communion.

"To find one's purpose," he'd said, *"is the greatest quest any man can make."*

Nick had leaned in, caught in the gravity of the moment. *"But, Papou, how will I know when I find my purpose?"*

Papou's smile was warm but sobering. *"Your purpose,"* he said, *"will require great courage, commitment, and perseverance. It will demand more from you than you think you can withstand."*

Nick remembered going quiet after that. He'd wanted to ask more, to press his grandfather on what kind of purpose would ask so much. But something in those words unsettled him. *More than you think you can withstand.* That didn't sound like adventure. That sounded like suffering. And suffering wasn't fun. So, he never asked.

Now, six decades later, with the weight of failure heavy on his shoulders and nothing but ashes where his empire used to be, Nick wished he'd asked more. The simplicity of his grandfather's truths echoed louder now than they ever had. Respect. Kindness. Hard work. Service. Love. Loyalty. Legacy.

He had respected, until he hadn't.

He had been kind until bitterness set in.

He had worked hard, but had he served anyone but himself?

Nick blew out a slow, deliberate plume of smoke, watching it fade into the still air. He could still hear Papou's voice, soft but resolute: "*To find one's purpose is the greatest quest…*"

Maybe that's why Nick felt so lost. Because he hadn't just lost a business, or money, or reputation, he had lost the quest. And somewhere in the blur of ambition and ego, he'd stopped looking for his purpose altogether.

* * *

Michele drew a long, slow breath as she watched him from the kitchen. There he was again at the bar, hunched over with a cigarette in one hand, the other curled around a glass of scotch. More time spent with his mistress. That's what she called them now—those damn cigarettes. They'd taken her place in the pecking order of his affections. She studied the way he handled them, so gently, so reverently. The way his fingers wrapped around them as though they were precious. The soft, practiced purse of his lips to draw in their toxic kiss. She hated them. Hated the smell, the way they clung to his clothes, to the air between them. But more than anything, she hated the space they created— the intimacy he reserved for a stick of nicotine instead of for her.

He used to touch me like that, she thought bitterly.

Michele yanked her gaze away before her fury boiled over. Her fingers twitched with the urge to unleash the full force of her frustration, to berate him for poisoning his body, for withdrawing, for becoming someone she barely recognised. But she didn't. Instead, her eyes landed on the red roses standing proud and fragrant in the crystal vase on the bench. They shone like a small victory, their beauty untainted. *Nature,* she thought, *knew how to demonstrate love.* Even if her husband had forgotten how.

She sighed. The sharp edge of her anger softened, dulled by the weight of compassion. She knew why he was like this. He was lost. Untethered. A man without a mission. A yacht without wind. And for a man like Nick, purpose wasn't just important—it was necessary for survival.

She'd tried to tell him. She'd said it more times than she could count: "*Help someone else. Serve. Give. That's the way out of this.*"

Gratitude, generosity, grace. Those were the keys. But every time she reached for him with wisdom, he recoiled like she'd slapped him. It was as if hearing the truth from her made it sting more.

Her mother's voice echoed in her mind, thick with that old-world certainty, "*You can take a horse to water, but you can't make it drink.*"

And Nick? He was one stubborn, cantankerous old stallion, hooves dug in, eyes wild, flanks heaving with pride. She chuckled at the thought, but the humour faded fast. Because deep down, she knew there was something else. Something darker than depression or purposelessness. Something troubled him that he had yet to confess. She could feel it, like a storm brewing just beyond the horizon.

He's hiding something, she thought. *Something heavy.*

And when it came, when he finally laid it bare, she feared it might break them both. That was the part that kept her up at night. Not the silence. Not even the slow decay of what they used to be. No... it was the knowing that when the truth came, it might be too much to bear.

CHAPTER THREE

Like most nights, Nick fell asleep on the couch or at least pretended to. It had become a silent ritual, his nightly performance of detachment. If he looked asleep, it spared them both the painful charade of closeness. No awkward pause in the hallway, no fumbling for a kiss that neither of them could make feel real anymore. Just the soft hush of her footsteps retreating toward the bedroom and the gentle click of the door as she shut him out. Or shut herself in.

When he heard it close, he exhaled and opened one eye. Another day survived. Another truth buried. Another lie added to the mountain of guilt crushing his chest like a slow, suffocating weight. He sat up, the room tilting slightly as he cupped his face in his hands. His palms were cold and clammy. Hands that had once clasped another's in agreement, signed contracts, and closed deals. Now they shook with exhaustion. With cowardice.

Tomorrow, he thought. *I'll tell her tomorrow.*

But he'd thought that yesterday and the day before. The truth loomed like a cliff edge, and he couldn't seem to find the courage to jump. Dragging his tired frame off the couch, he shuffled down the hallway like a man twice his age. Every step was an echo of pain. His shoulder still ached from that fall on the stairs. The scar from his minor operation twinged, and his knees cracked and moaned like rusty hinges. This year had been nothing but one damn thing after another: illnesses, injuries, strange little malfunctions of the body. And Michele, bless her soul, could find divine meaning in every ache and pain.

She'd explained each one with that calm certainty of hers. "*Shoulder pain—you're carrying burdens not meant for you. Stomach—you're digesting guilt. Skin issues—emotional boundaries.*" God, she was relentless. Relentless and *usually right.*

She was smart like that. Too smart. So finely tuned to her inner voice, to energy, to patterns that most people missed entirely. Somewhere in that sixth sense of hers,

Nick knew she already knew. Even if he hadn't spoken the words aloud, she could feel the truth because that's who Michele was. She felt people. She read them. Him most of all. But he had hidden it. Somehow, he'd kept the mask in place, the facade intact. Still, the part that chilled him most wasn't that he'd lied. It was that he'd broken the promise that had formed the sacred core of their bond.

Truth. Always the truth.

As he slid into the cold, crisp sheets of the spare bed, even this felt like an admission of guilt.

Truth. Always the truth.

No matter how hard, how humiliating, how shattering, it had been their vow from the start. She had kept hers. Of that, he had no doubt. Michele couldn't lie to save her life. Even if she tried, it showed in her eyes, in her hands, in the way her voice betrayed her. As a child, she'd been the good girl, the peacekeeper, the light in her parents' storm. She'd made a mission out of bringing joy, of doing right. Honesty wasn't just a virtue for her. It was a way of being.

He remembered that exercise they'd done years ago where they ranked their values. Hers had been clear: Love. Spiritual growth. Truth. Top three. No hesitation. His list had looked different. Money. Success. Freedom. Truth had been there, but not high enough. Not until he saw how much it mattered to her. That was when he shifted. Recalibrated. Recommitted. But promises made in the sunlight of love often broke in the shadows of shame.

Now, lying there in the dark, he stared up at the ceiling, heart thudding in the silence. The room felt heavier than usual, as if the truth had grown thick enough to take up space. He could hear her voice in his head, like a soft chant from another world.

"Nick… the truth will set you free. Tell me," Michele had said, time and again.

God, how he hated that quote tonight. Hated that it was hers. Hated that it was right. The words rang through him, not angry, not accusing. Just sad. Tired. Like her.

He groaned, rolling onto his side, pulling the covers over his head as if they might muffle the voice of his own conscience. He didn't want freedom. Not if it came with that look on her face—that pain in her eyes. Tonight, like so many nights before, he prayed, not for redemption, but for release.

"Let me sleep forever," he whispered into the void. "Let me disappear."

Because death, in all its finality, seemed kinder than confession.

* * *

WITH THE SUN filtering through the thin curtains, so too arrived another day of indecision. The light was soft, almost forgiving, but it didn't fool Nick. Daylight only meant one thing: more time to wrestle with what he knew he had to do and still couldn't bring himself to face. He lay there for a few seconds, staring at the ceiling like it might offer him an answer. It didn't. What he needed first was a heart starter—coffee and a cigarette. Michele wouldn't be up for another half-hour at least. She liked to take her time waking slowly, stretching gently like a cat in a sunbeam. He, on the other hand, felt like a bear climbing out of a cave.

He threw on yesterday's clothes and headed out to the summer house. Morning dew clung to the air, but it was already warming. He made a strong, black, bitter coffee, took a sip, and lit his first cigarette of the day. That first inhale was like an old friend who never judged, never asked questions. Just showed up and gave him a moment of respite. He was about to light a second one when his phone buzzed beside him. He glanced at the screen. Theo. A small smile tugged at Nick's mouth.

"*Hey, Mate,*" came the familiar voice, bright and breezy, cutting through the morning haze like sunshine. "*How's it going?*"

Nick exhaled, trying to muster a convincing tone. "Hey. Not bad."

"*Bullshit.*" Theo didn't even skip a beat. "*What's wrong?*"

Nick huffed a short laugh. If there was one person he couldn't bluff, it was Theo: his oldest mate, his best mate. They'd been through just about everything together—pub brawls, heartbreaks, business deals, drinking trips where they'd shared more truths over beer than they ever had stone-cold sober. Nick acquiesced and gave him the rundown. Not every gritty detail, just enough to paint the picture. Enough to show how deep he was in. There was a pause on the line, the kind that only happens between friends who don't need filler words. Then, just as expected, came the verdict.

"*Mate… you tell her, and it's over.*"

Nick winced. The words hit hard, even though he knew they were coming. "You sure about that?"

"*C'mon. Every bloke I know who's fessed up about that kind of thing has either lost the house, the dog, or his bloody balls. Sometimes all three.*"

Nick gave a half-laugh, but it was hollow.

"*Let sleeping dogs lie,*" another mate had told Nick last week, beer in hand, voice laced with the kind of resignation Nick had seen too often lately.

"*If you don't want to lose everything, keep your mouth shut.*"

He'd heard it all. The chorus of caution. The man-code of silence.

But none of them were married to Michele. "She's not like that," Nick said, mostly to himself.

"*What's that?*" said Theo.

Nick cleared his throat. "I've never lied to her. Not once in all our years. I never have. Until now. And it's fucking killing me."

Another pause.

"*Well… you know what I think. Shit. You're a bigger man than me if you do. It'll take some serious balls on your part.*"

Nick gave a half-smirk, dropping a hand absentmindedly to his crotch. Unconsciously, he did a quick check. "Yeah," he muttered, "I know."

There was a light chuckle on the other end. "*Good luck, mate. You'll need it.*"

"Thanks for the call. I'll let you know what happens."

Theo's voice dropped to a mock-dramatic tone. "*Okay, but do me a favour first. Remove all sharp objects from the house and hide that cast-iron frying pan. You know the one.*"

Nick laughed despite himself. "You're a prick."

"*Damn right.*"

The call ended with Theo's hearty chuckle still ringing in his ear, leaving Nick alone with his cooling coffee, half-smoked cigarette, and the same old ache in his chest. He sat back, dragging a slow inhale.

You're a bigger man than me if you do.

Nick wasn't so sure he was. He felt smaller by the day. But he also felt that today might just be different. Maybe.

Realising Michele still hadn't surfaced, Nick stubbed out his cigarette and wandered down the winding path to the lower garden. The scent of orange blossom hung in the air, mingling with the salt breeze drifting in from the Pacific. He and Michele had spent years designing and cultivating every inch of the property. Each tree, each tropical plant, each meandering path told a story. They'd shaped the land as much as it had shaped them. And scattered throughout it were little corners of quietude, sanctuary spaces Michele had insisted on. Places to sit, reflect, write, and pray.

She called them "soul spaces." He used to tease her about them; back in the early days, when her devotion to some higher power had amused him. Her talk of guides, spirit conversations, God, and consciousness had sounded like mystic mumbo jumbo to a man raised on hard logic and grit. But over time, her unwavering faith, her peace, her grace had softened something in him. He might never have sat cross-legged beside her or joined her in meditation, but he'd come to believe there was something more out there. Something science couldn't measure. A Presence. An Intelligence. Something sacred.

Today, though… today felt different. As he wandered past each of the garden's sacred nooks, something tugged at him, an invisible thread pulling him inward. Without knowing why, he turned toward one of the more secluded spots, a small sanctuary nestled in the crook of a bamboo grove. It was one of Michele's favourites; a curved stone bench shaded by whispering green, where the breeze always seemed gentler. He paused, glancing around as if expecting someone to stop him. But there wasn't anyone. Just sunlight, birdsong, and the rhythmic hush of waves. With a sheepish shrug to no one in particular, he sat. The stone was solid and cool beneath him.

He perched upright, unsure of what to do with his hands. Then he closed his eyes, cautiously at first. He hated closing his eyes while awake. It made him feel vulnerable, like he was inviting the unknown too close. But now, something inside him needed this stillness. His breathing slowed. His shoulders dropped. For the first time in ages, Nick allowed his thoughts to dissolve like sea foam. And in that quiet, so complete, so uncharacteristic, an old memory floated to the surface.

He was a boy again beside his Papou in the Greek Orthodox church. The thick smell of beeswax candles, the hollow echo of the priest's voice through the stone sanctuary, the hush of reverence. He saw himself guiding his blind grandfather to the vestibule, helping him light a candle. The flame flickered to life like a secret promise. Then they walked down the aisle, hand to elbow, to sit at the end of the pew. Nick remembered the way Papou would nod as the word of God was proclaimed, his sightless eyes turned toward the altar like he could see something no one else could.

And then, as clearly as if he were sitting beside him now, Papou spoke. "*Tell her, Nikos. She will forgive you.*"

Nick's eyes flew open. His heart leapt to his throat.

"*Tell her, Nikos. Tell her now.*"

The voice was unmistakable. Calm, gentle, firm. Papou's voice.

Nick whipped his head around, scanning the garden, but of course, there was no one there. Just wind stirring the bamboo and the far-off sigh of waves caressing the shore.

"Papou?" Nick whispered. "Was that you?"

Silence. But it didn't matter. In that moment, something shifted inside him. A spark of certainty ignited in the pit of his belly. With it, a jolt of courage he hadn't felt in months. It was a sign. He was sure of it. He stood, exhaled, and nodded to no one and everyone. He knew not only what he had to do, but that he could do it. He glanced down, adjusted his stance, and gave his crotch a quick, affirming tug.

"Let's go, fellas," he muttered. "It's now or never."

With that, Nick turned toward the house, toward Michele, and toward the truth, whatever it might bring.

CHAPTER FOUR

MICHELE PADDED AROUND THE HOUSE, barefoot and unhurried. The morning light spilled through the windows like liquid gold, casting soft shadows across the floor. Nick's car was still parked in the garage, so he had to be somewhere on the property. She called his name once, then again, but not too loudly. She quite liked having the house to herself in the early hours. When he wasn't physically present, his heavy energy didn't press in quite so tightly. It lingered, clinging to corners like smoke after a fire, but it wasn't overpowering. And she'd become quite adept at clearing it with a little sage and intention during her cleansing ritual after he left the house.

She paused at the kitchen bench and smiled to no one in particular. "I'm going to make myself a cappuccino and finish reading my book," she declared aloud, her tone light, purposeful.

The mere thought of such a simple pleasure lifted her spirits, like a small kite caught in a warm breeze. She turned on the coffee machine, its familiar hum grounding her. Then she opened the cupboard and chose her favourite cup and saucer—a delicate porcelain set Nick had given her years ago. The one with the soft golden sheen covering the cup and the hand-painted reflective saucer. She used to feel a pang when she reached for it, a bittersweet ache for what they used to be. But today she didn't feel the melancholy rise. Instead, she felt a warm pulse of peace in her chest, as if something within her had shifted while she slept.

As the machine hissed to life, she closed her eyes and mentally recited her morning gratitude practice. One by one, the affirmations rolled silently from her lips like prayer beads sliding through her fingers.

Thank you for this new day. Thank you for my perfect health, wealth, and happiness. Thank you for guiding me on my path and for the opportunities presented to me along the way. I am safe. I am at peace. I am prosperous.

With each phrase, her energy lifted. She could feel herself climbing the emotional scale—out of worry, out of weariness, into something softer, lighter, steadier.

By the time she finished frothing the milk and placed her cup on its matching saucer, her whole body buzzed with quiet joy. She carried her cappuccino outside to the summer house overlooking the garden, the sacred space she'd created just for mornings like this. The ocean sparkled in the distance. Birds chirped their melodies as if the entire day had joined her in celebration. Michele settled onto the daybed, drew her knees up, and wrapped a soft throw around her legs. Steam rose from her coffee in little swirls, and she breathed it in like incense. She didn't know where Nick was, or what kind of mood he'd be in when he appeared, but she didn't need to. Today, she chose light. She chose joy. She chose *herself.*

Start the day on the front foot. Get out ahead of it. Everything always works out for me.

The words echoed in her mind. A sacred promise she made to herself every morning. And today, more than ever, they felt true. Something was shifting. She could feel it, not in her bones, but in her spirit. Nick was coming closer to truth, and she would be ready.

* * *

NICK ROUNDED THE corner and froze. There she was, sitting in the soft light of morning, her fingers wrapped around the cup, steam rising in gentle spirals. The sun caught her hair, setting it aglow like strands of gold. She looked peaceful. Serene. Beautiful in a way that almost undid him. Lovelier, even, than the day he'd married her. A lump rose in his throat, thick and merciless. How could he do this to her? More importantly, how had he done it at all? His stomach churned, and he could almost hear the stone of his guilt dropping into it, the thud reverberating through his bones. Every inch of him recoiled.

"*Tell her, Nikos.*" Papou's voice rang again, firm and quiet in his mind.

His feet moved forward, but it felt like walking through wet concrete. Each step was an anchor, dragging the weight of every lie behind him. By the time he stood just beyond arm's reach, his body trembled, whether from fear, grief, or shame, he didn't know. He tried to summon a smile, something casual, nonchalant, but the muscles in his face refused to obey.

"I have something to tell you," he said, voice low, cracked. There it was. The moment. No turning back. The die had been cast.

Michele looked up at him and smiled softly, lovingly. "Of course. Sit with me." She shifted over, making space for him, space he declined because he didn't deserve.

"I think it's better if I stand."

She paused, something in her stilling. She placed the cup and saucer on the side table and turned to face him. Her head tilted, a gesture of innocent, unguarded curiosity.

She has no idea. And that broke him most of all.

"I've done something…" he started, but his throat clamped shut. The words lodged there, barbed and bitter. He tried to swallow, but his mouth was a desert. He forced breath through his nose.

"Go on," she said.

He noticed the tension in her body shift, subtle but certain. She was listening with her whole being, he knew it. He drew a breath. "I've been having an affair." The words landed like a grenade in a cathedral. Everything sacred shattered. The silence that followed wasn't just still. It was obliteration. The entire world disappeared beneath it.

Michele blinked once, twice. A small, involuntary shake of her head followed, like someone waking from a dream. "What?"

Nick couldn't move. He stood there, head bowed, ashamed beyond measure.

"I've been having an affair for the past five months," he said again, quieter. "I'm so sorry." The shame blanketed him. His shoulders curled forward like a man awaiting a blow. Every nerve screamed to run, to escape, but he didn't move. He stood. He would take what came.

Michele rose with slow, eerie grace. She straightened, unfolding like a sail unfurling in a storm. "You what?" Her voice cracked. "What did you say?"

He opened his mouth to answer, but the words dissolved. *Coward.*

"What do you mean you had an affair?" Her voice, sharper, climbing in pitch. "When? With who? What the fuck, Nick?"

And then she screamed—raw, primal, the sound of a soul being split. *"Five. Fucking Months!"*

Her voice pierced through his chest like a blade, and then she was in motion. She shoved past him, rage surging in her every step as she strode toward the house.

Numb, he watched her go. For a split second, he thought to follow her, to offer… what? An apology? A hand? A thread of comfort?

She turned, her face a mask of rage, as he took a single step forward. All the light in her had vanished. In its place: Fire. Contempt. Fury. Betrayal.

"Don't you dare come near me," she snarled, her voice trembling with the magnitude of her rage. "If you follow me, I swear to God… I'll take a knife to you." She spat the words like venom. "Stay away from me. Get out of this house."

Nick recoiled, jaw slack, vanquished. He watched her disappear into the house, her energy trailing behind her like choking fumes. The air around him felt scorched. He stood there—a man undone. He had loved her. He loved her still. Yet, he had become the architect of her undoing. Like Dr. Frankenstein, he had breathed life into a monster, but the monster wasn't Michele.

It was him. And this? This was his penance.

* * *

Michele flew through the house like a woman possessed. And she was possessed. Possessed by her worst nightmare made flesh. The very thing she'd feared in fleeting shadows now stood before her in stark daylight, speaking with Nick's voice, wearing Nick's face. She had always prided herself on her ability to regulate emotion. Decades of meditation and spiritual discipline had made her a master of calm, a beacon of poise. But nothing had prepared her for this. Nothing for the speed at which betrayal could rip through her like a cyclone. Nothing for the violence of the thoughts now swamping her mind. It was as though something ancient and ferocious had been unleashed inside her, something primal and unhinged.

Navigating the kitchen, she glanced toward the knife block. *So, this is how normal, sane women kill their husbands,* she thought. *This is how the line gets crossed.*

If he had followed her, if he had dared to come one step closer, she would've driven a blade through his disgusting, traitorous heart and not regretted it for a second. She thundered into the bedroom and slammed the door so hard it reverberated through the walls, clapping like a divine gavel. Pacing like a caged animal, cornered and confused, she tried to digest the words that still echoed in her ears.

He's been having an affair. For five months. Five fucking months.

While she had held him through his despair. While she had prayed for him, meditated for him, and begged the Universe to help him. While she had poured herself out in every possible way, he had been curled in the arms of another woman. Her throat clenched; her skin prickled with rage. She grabbed their wedding photo from the dresser, stared for one agonizing second into the eyes of the man she thought she knew, and then hurled it against the wall. The frame exploded, a burst of glass and crystal shards, pieces of their marriage scattered across the floor.

From somewhere deep within, beyond her control, came a sound. A wail. Long, guttural, inhuman. It tore from her throat like the roar of a wounded animal, stilling her as she bellowed her agony to the heavens. The next moment, she was pacing again, her heart pounding, her thoughts spinning, connecting dots with terrifying clarity. The distance between them. The sudden revulsion to touch. The constant criticism. The nights away. Not with his mates but with… her… that bitch! Michele's fists clenched, nails digging into her palms, ready to draw blood. Her breath came in fast bursts, ragged and burning, like fire being forced through a straw. She turned on her heel, possessed by fury, and stormed out of the bedroom.

She spotted him outside, still standing there, like a statue.

Her fists raised, and with a cry that could have split the heavens, she launched toward him. "You fucking liar! You fucking liar!" she screamed, pounding her fists against his chest, again and again. "I asked you! I asked you what was wrong. I asked if you were having an affair!" Her voice fractured, but the rage kept rising. "And you lied. You lied!"

Each blow she landed was powered by disbelief, betrayal, and heartbreak. She needed him to feel it. To know what he had done. Not intellectually. But viscerally in every part of his body. He didn't stop her. He didn't flinch. He just stood there, slack-jawed, hollow. Letting her rage pour over him.

"You murdered us," she cried, tears breaking free. "You murdered our marriage."

And then, it left her. All the rage, all the fury, drained from her in an instant, like a dam breaking. Her arms dropped to her sides. Her breathing slowed. Her body began to tremble. The sobs came hard and fast, from a place so deep she hadn't even known it existed. Michele crumpled to the floor at his feet, her hands covering her face, her voice barely a whisper now.

"You murdered me... you murdered me... you murdered me."

Nick knelt silently beside her and wrapped his arms around her heaving shoulders. He said nothing. And there, amid the wreckage of truth, they huddled, broken and breathless, rocking gently to the far-off rhythm of waves kissing the shore. Two souls adrift in the aftermath of betrayal, unsure whether they were holding on to each other or to the last fragile threads of what used to be.

CHAPTER FIVE

A BROKEN MAN, SOUL LAID bare, Nick cradled his wife in his arms, unable to offer any solace. What comfort could he possibly give? He was the cause of her unimaginable pain. The architect of the implosion. The one who had taken their sacred promise and shattered it, over and over again. He had lied. Repeatedly. He had murdered the marriage they had so carefully built, piece by loving piece. Now, he had no idea how to bring it back to life. Would she even want to try? Would she ever consider resuscitation? Or had he cut too deep, gone too far? He had thrown the chips in the air. Now he could do nothing but wait and see where they fell.

Michele thrashed out of his arms, every movement sharp and wild. "Get out!" she snarled, voice laced with venom. "Get out of this house. Go to your fucking little whore mistress. We're through."

She launched to her feet, towering over him like a tempest, screaming down through her tears. "*Get out!*"

Then she was gone, fleeing toward the house, hurling curses over her shoulder like arrows, each one piercing the remnants of his resolve. Nick remained on the ground for a moment, stunned by the weight of her fury, the absolute finality in her voice. He didn't want to leave. He didn't want to let go. He wanted to fix it. Somehow. He loved her. Dear God, he loved her. But he'd made a mistake. The biggest mistake of his life. And he knew it might have cost him everything.

"*Let her be, Nikos.*" The voice returned. Steady. Soft. His Papou again.

Nick nodded in agreement, the words settling over him like a soothing balm. He dragged himself upright, legs unsteady beneath the weight of shame, and made his way to his cigarettes. His pacifier. His poison. Lighting one with a shaky hand, he inhaled deeply, as though the smoke might dull the edge of everything. It might buy him a moment of quiet in the storm of self-loathing. He strained to organise his thoughts, to upregulate his emotions, to find even a flicker of light in what now felt like a pitch-black tunnel. But there was nothing. Just ash. Just the thick, sour taste of regret. He had betrayed the one person in his life who had never betrayed him.

Nick knew betrayal. His father had betrayed him. His mother. His brother. The extended Greek chorus of aunts and cousins who'd turned their backs when it mattered most. Friends.

Business partners. Loyal until loyalty became inconvenient or costly. Yes... Nick knew betrayal intimately. He had lived inside it. He had felt the sting of it again and again, until it etched itself into the marrow of his bones. Yet here he stood—the worst betrayer of all.

He took another drag, deeper this time, letting the burn fill his lungs. A pathetic attempt to suffocate the truth. But it wouldn't die.

Michele was right. He had murdered their marriage. He had destroyed the best part of them both. He decided he could at least do what she'd asked of him now. He stubbed out his cigarette, the ember dying with a faint hiss, like a final breath. For a moment, he just stood there, the silence pressing in, heavy and absolute. Then, shoulders slumped, soul hollowed out, he turned toward the house; not as a husband returning, but as a man exiled. There would be no grand gesture. No plea for forgiveness. Just quiet obedience. He would pack his things, and he would get out.

* * *

EVEN FROM A young age, crying had been Michele's medicine. Tears had always brought her relief, not weakness, not indulgence, but relief. A sacred offering to the pain, a coming home to herself, creating space for light to return. As if to validate what her body had always known, science had finally caught up, proving that crying held powerful physiological and emotional healing properties. It reset the nervous system and softened the jagged edges of trauma. Now, with the storm spent and her body limp from the emotional purge, she sat quietly on the edge of the bed. Her breath now moved more smoothly through her chest. The raw shock of Nick's betrayal had dulled just enough to allow clarity to begin its return.

All those decades of meditation, of inner listening, of centred stillness, were finally paying their dues. She breathed herself back into balance. Not perfectly, but enough. She reconnected with the deeper part of her that had never been betrayed. The part of her that knew peace was a practice, not a place.

She had been betrayed before, professionally in her career and personally by friends. But this time, it was by the man she loved. The man she trusted most of all. Yet he had betrayed her. But she would not betray herself. She reminded herself of one of the hardest universal truths, one she had taught to others a hundred times, but which now required her full embodiment: *What appears to be happening is only my perception of reality.*

Difficult as it was to swallow, she knew that reality was never fixed. It bent and curved according to our consciousness. Quantum physics proved it.

Change your state. Change your fate.

It didn't make the betrayal any easier to digest, but it did make it possible to consider her next move from a place of alignment rather than anguish. Over the years, in her work and her life, Michele had lived by what she called the Faith Formula: a quiet but powerful compass that had guided her through countless storms.

Truth + Transparency = Trust
Trust10 = Faith

Faith was not just belief. It was knowing without evidence. A frequency she chose to embody, even when the facts tried to shout it down.

And Nick? Nick had failed on all three counts. He had not told her the truth. He had not been transparent. And because of that, trust, once the very foundation of their union, had crumbled.

She'd known something was wrong long before he spoke the words. Her inner guidance had whispered, then prodded, then screamed. And in a moment of desperation, she'd done something she'd never done before in all their years together. She'd checked his appointment diary. That act alone had felt like a violation. But it had also felt necessary. A last-ditch attempt to validate what her intuition already knew. Of course, she'd found nothing. Nick was too smart for that. Too cunning. Especially when it came to covering his tracks. But the damage was already done—not by what she found, but by what she felt.

Those initial niggles had intensified into distrust. The distrust had quickly twisted into distorted thinking, imagining scenarios, filling in gaps. And then had come the disappointment. Sharp. Soul-deep. The slow disintegration of connection, long before either of them had named it. Still… an affair? No matter how strained things had become, Michele never imagined that would be part of their story. There was no excuse—not in her world. And yet, here they were.

Now was not the time for depression. Now was the time for decision. Now was the time for discipline—of thought, of emotion, of energy. She would not let this moment drag her into bitterness. She would rise. She must rise. But she needed clarity. Questions needed answering. Not for the sake of punishment, but for understanding. Closure. Healing. She could not move forward, spiritually or emotionally, without those truths.

And only Nick could provide them. After months of lies and deception, could he finally tell her the truth? She had no way of knowing. But there was no alternative. She would face him head-on, not from a place of collapse, but from the power of her centre. Her truth was clear. Her guidance had returned. And she would follow it, one step at a time, toward whatever came next.

Gathering herself, Michele returned to the bathroom. Her legs still trembled slightly, her hands not quite steady, but her will had returned. The first wave of grief had crashed, and though her heart was still splintered, she would not allow herself to remain collapsed beneath the wreckage. She stood in front of the mirror, staring at her own reflection as though trying to remember who she was before this. Mascara streaked down her cheeks like war paint, her hair tousled, her lips pale.

No, she thought. *Not like this. Not now.*

She grabbed a tissue and wiped the dark trails from her skin, pulled her hair back into something resembling order, and reached for her lipstick. A sweep of colour across her lips. A symbol, if nothing else. A mask, yes—but her mask. Her armour. She would not face him as a shattered woman. She would face him as herself, whole, wise, and done with being deceived.

When she stepped into the hallway, she felt taller. Stronger. She found him in the spare bedroom, hunched over an open suitcase. His movements were slow, like a man moving through quicksand. When he lifted his head and saw her, there was no anger in his face, just quiet devastation.

"I'm doing what you asked," he said.

Michele stood in the doorway, her arms crossed loosely, the distance between them echoing with unspoken history. She didn't step forward. She didn't soften. Her eyes locked onto his like twin blades. "Good," she said. Her voice was even but laced with steel. "But first, I have a few questions I need answered."

Nick nodded.

She took a breath, her tone sharpening. "Even though you've proved yourself to be a pathological liar, do you think you could manage to tell the truth this time?" She hadn't meant for it to come out with such venom, but the words had a life of their own. Truthfully, she was entitled. She was the one who'd been betrayed. He was the one who had broken everything.

Nick turned to face her fully. His expression was unreadable. "Ask whatever you want," he said. "I'll tell you whatever you want to know."

"Right," she said, her voice clear, unwavering. "Who is she? And how did all this start?"

CHAPTER SIX

" *T*ELL HER, NIKOS. *She will forgive you.*"
        Papou's voice echoed in Nick's head like a bell tolling in a distant village. But where once those words felt like guidance, now they sounded like a cruel joke. Forgiveness? He couldn't even imagine it. Not after what he'd seen in Michele's eyes, shock, hurt, and betrayal so raw it had sucked the air out of the room. He hadn't just broken her heart. He had shattered the foundation they'd built their lives on.

Yet here she stood, arms crossed, eyes burning, her jaw set. She was going to demand answers, real answers. And he would have to give them. Answers to questions he didn't want to say out loud, because saying them would make everything even more real. Saying them would confirm, beyond any shadow of doubt, what kind of man he'd become. He understood why she needed the truth. He even respected it. But how he hated himself for being the one to deliver pain wrapped in honesty. Still, it was time. No more lies. No more dodging.

The whole truth and nothing but the truth. Help me, God.

He swallowed hard, throat dry as gravel, and longed for the comfort of a cigarette. But instead, he stood there, raw, exposed, the man who'd torn everything apart. "We met at a conference at the beginning of the year," he began, eyes locked on the floor. "I didn't mean for anything to happen. But as you know, I struggled with losing the business, my family, and everything else. I wasn't in a good place… and one thing led to another…"

"One thing does not lead to another," Michele snapped, slicing his excuse in half. "This was an affair, Nick. Not a one-night lapse in judgement. You didn't stumble. You chose. Again, and again. You made a conscious decision to break your vows and keep breaking them. For five *months. Five months!*"

He winced, her words landing like hammer blows to his chest. "I know," he said. "But it's been over for a while now."

"There are no buts." Her voice cracked. "And it hasn't been over. Not for *me*. You've been walking around like a fucking bear with a sore head, snapping at everything, sulking in silence. You brought it home. Every. Single. Day."

Nick felt the truth of her words like nails driving into flesh. "I swear. I ended it months ago. I just… I didn't know how to tell you. I'm so sorry, Michele. I'm so sorry for everything." His voice broke, the words spilling out like something rotten. He sounded pathetic, like the weasel he knew he was. Desperate to be forgiven for something he couldn't even justify.

Michele didn't flinch. She didn't comfort. She was the storm now, composed yet full of fury. "Who was she?" she asked. "What's her name?"

Nick's stomach dropped. God. She wanted everything.

"Tell her, Nikos. She will forgive you."

He didn't believe it anymore. If Papou's voice was anything, maybe it was just his mind clinging to a thread of false hope. Or worse, temptation, like the devil whispering in the desert. Maybe this was his desert. His exile. His punishment. Exactly what he deserved. He dragged in a long, slow breath, pretending it was a cigarette, and forced himself to answer.

"Her name was Joanna."

Michele blinked. "How old was she?"

"Forty-seven."

He watched as she reached out, her fingers brushing the door frame like she needed something solid to hold on to.

"That's the same age as your daughter," she said, her voice somewhere between a scoff and a sob. "What in the world would a forty-seven-year-old woman want with an old man like you?"

The sting was instant.

"She must have some serious issues with men," Michele continued, her words now a scalpel. "Or daddy issues. Couldn't find someone her own age? Because you're no Pierce Brosnan, Nick. Not even close." She looked him over with an expression so sharp it could have drawn blood. "She must've thought you had money. Boy, she played you, buddy."

Each word felt like it split him in two. But she wasn't wrong. She never was when it came to reading people.

Maybe that was the worst part. She still saw right through him.

Michele extended her hand suddenly. "Is she in your phone? Show me."

Nick hesitated, but only for a moment. He didn't dare defy her. He opened his contacts, found Joanna's name, and handed over the phone with a sick sense of surrender.

She studied the contact. Tapped the photo. Curled her lip in disgust. "And you jeopardised everything we had— for this?"

Right again. Michele was in a league of her own. Maybe that was it. Maybe he'd spent all these years secretly believing he was batting above his weight. Maybe he had finally given up and chosen someone lesser because he felt lesser. Because some part of him had stopped believing he was worthy of a woman like Michele. He didn't know. He couldn't make sense of it. He just wanted this inquisition to end.

"I'm so sorry," he said again, hollow. "It was stupid. I was stupid. I was just so miserable… I just…" His voice trailed off. There was no good ending to that sentence. Nothing he could say that wouldn't sound like a bad excuse for an inexcusable choice. Standing there, face to face with the woman he'd betrayed, Nick finally realised how far he'd fallen. And just how far there might be to climb back, if climbing back was even possible.

Handing back the phone, Michele's eyes didn't leave his. "Call her," she said, cool and calm as ice, though her tone left no room for negotiation. "On hands-free. I want to speak with her."

Holy fuck.

Nick had known Michele was tough. She didn't flinch at life's messiness. She faced down grief, stood tall through betrayals in her own life, and navigated storms with that quiet grace of hers. But this? He hadn't seen this coming.

"You want to talk to her?" he asked, his voice dry, a note of incredulity hanging in the air.

Michele didn't speak. She just glared, a silent, unmoving force of nature, and gave a single nod.

Nick hesitated, then pressed the call button, his thumb trembling. He placed the call on speaker, the room seeming to tighten around him as the phone rang.

Then: "*Hello? I haven't heard from you for a while.*" Joanna's voice, light and vaguely flirty, echoed into the room like a ghost Nick had buried and hoped never to unearth. At least her greeting worked in his favour. It confirmed he had ended things months ago.

Nick cleared his throat. "I've got Michele here. I've told her everything. She wants to talk to you." His hand shook as he passed the phone over.

Michele's didn't. Her grip was steady. Strong. Unflinching. "I hear you've been having an affair with my husband," she said, her voice measured, elegant, surgical.

Nick nearly applauded her. This was Michele in full flight: dignified, direct, lethal with language. He'd always admired that about her. And in this moment, he feared it.

A pause on the other end. Then, Joanna responded, "*No. He's been having an affair with me,*" she said, her tone puffed with righteousness, as if staking a claim.

Bad move. Nick braced.

"Don't play semantics with me," Michele snapped, her voice now sharp enough to slice glass.

Another beat. Then Joanna replied, almost sanctimoniously, "*Well, it's over. Perhaps this is a good opportunity for the two of you to work it out.*"

Nick's hands twitched at his sides, instinctively wanting to shield his head. *She's going to blow.*

And blow she did.

"How dare you!" Michele erupted, her tone volcanic, ripping through the air like thunder. "What right do you have to tell me anything? You know nothing! And why would I want to 'work anything out' with a lying, cheating betrayer like him?" She stabbed at the phone, ending the call in one furious motion, and flung it onto the bed as if the device itself was contaminated. "Remove her from your contacts."

Nick didn't hesitate. He obeyed, fingers fumbling over the screen, finding the contact and deleting it.

But Michele wasn't done. "Just so you know," she said, eyes narrowing, "I don't trust you. I know you can retrieve it. You probably have her stored everywhere—WhatsApp, Signal, wherever else you crawled off to deceive me. But know this. I'll know. I always do."

Nick nodded silently, the shame settling deeper into his gut. He wanted to thank her, absurd as it sounded. Not for the rage, but for the call. For making it final. For shutting the door on Joanna, who had become unhinged after he ended the affair. There had been calls at all hours—voice messages thick with desperation—the Glenn Close *"Fatal Attraction"* kind. He half-expected to find a boiled rabbit in the pot one day.

Michele was right. *How the hell had he attracted a 'rabbit cooker'?*

He stared down at the floor, trying to count the mistakes that had led him to this moment. He stopped counting. It didn't matter anymore. What mattered now was what came next and whether he had even the faintest chance of earning a second chance. As he stood there, waiting for Michele's next question or her verdict, Nick noticed something shift. Her shoulders, rigid with fury just moments before, softened. Just a little. A fractional easing he wouldn't have caught if he hadn't been staring at her with his whole heart.

Maybe… maybe there's a sliver of hope.

Michele exhaled sharply, gathering herself. She stepped forward, arms crossing her chest, her stance commanding but not cruel. "Right," she said, voice clipped but controlled. "Let's get a few things clear."

Nick braced himself.

"Because of all this, this globalist agenda and Covid bullshit, you've been moping around here for years," she said, her words landing like drumbeats. "You've lost direction. You've lost your purpose. And instead of fighting for yourself—for us—you let yourself sink deeper into depression."

She paused, staring him down. "Even with everything I told you, everything I tried to show you, you didn't listen. You didn't heed the signs. And now look where we are. Look where it's landed you. Landed us."

Nick lowered his head; the truth of it stung more than any slap could have. Her assessment was accurate. Brutally so. Though her words dampened the little flicker of hope trying to rise in him, he didn't blame her. She was right.

Michele continued, voice gaining momentum, "The worst part, Nick, is that you were willing to fight with me, but you weren't willing to fight for us."

She took a step closer. Her voice cracked, but she pressed on. "You just gave up. You surrendered to your own misery. Where is the man I married? The man who was intelligent, strong, cocky, who would step up no matter how hard life got? Where did he go?"

Nick shrugged helplessly, shame pooling in his gut. "This isn't an excuse," he said, voice hoarse, "but I was lonely. I didn't think you loved me anymore. You didn't want me to come near you, so I…"

"For fuck's sake, Nick," Michele barked, cutting him off. "Grow up. Why would I want you near me when you were angry all the time? You were unbearable to live with! I told you that!"

She was pacing now, her hands slicing through the air. "I suggested marriage counselling. You refused. I suggested you see a psychologist. You refused. I suggested we go out more, see friends, reconnect. You refused!"

Every word was a whip crack. "Everything I suggested to get us back on track, you shut down. And then you go and do this." She gestured between them, the space now thick with broken promises.

She stopped pacing, planting herself firmly in front of him, hands on her hips, foot tapping impatiently. "What the fuck did you think would happen, Nick?"

He stared at the floor, searching for words that didn't sound pathetic. "It's obvious… I didn't think." He lifted his eyes, pleading. "But at least I confessed. My mates told me not to." The second it left his mouth, he knew he'd thrown gasoline on the fire.

Michele's eyes narrowed to slits. She pounced. "Really?" she said, voice dripping with contempt. "And who would they be?"

Nick opened his mouth to answer, but she shook her head before he could form a syllable.

"Forget it," she snapped. "It doesn't matter. Men are all the same. Lie with other women, then close ranks and lie about it to their wives. Pack mentality."

The words stung. But he took it. He deserved it. In a sheepish tone, Nick tried again, more desperate now. "Look, I know I fucked up. I know I did. But I told you. Not soon enough, I know… but I did tell you. I've felt sick about it for months. I couldn't live with myself." He swallowed hard. "I know it's probably too late… but I'm willing to do whatever it takes to fix this. Anything you want. Just name it."

A heavy pause settled between them. A silence so dense, time slowed. And in that stillness, Nick felt something shift. Not forgiveness. Not absolution. But a softening. A space opening. He pressed on, heart hammering against his ribs. "I don't want to go, Michele. I want to stay. I want to see if we can make this work." He stepped closer, his voice dropping to a near whisper. "You have every right to be angry. Be angry at me for the rest of your life if you have to. I'll take it. I'll take whatever you need to give me. I deserve it."

His hands trembled at his sides. "But please… let me be here. Let me stay and try to rebuild what I broke. Even if you hate me forever. Even if I fail." He swallowed against the lump rising in his throat. "Please, Michele… let me try."

Another long pause stretched between them, taut and fragile. But this time, the silence wasn't filled with accusation. It was filled with something else. *Possibility.* It wasn't forgiveness. Not yet. It wasn't a clean slate. But it was a first step. Nick stood there, holding his breath, afraid to move, afraid even to hope too much.

Would she change her mind? Would she give him a second chance?

CHAPTER SEVEN

IT WAS AS IF MICHELE had split into two people. The one standing here, holding court with Nick, was her avatar, the polished surface self, taking charge, commanding the conversation, maintaining control. But behind that avatar lived her deeper self, the quieter Michele. The one tethered to universal wisdom, the one who knew how to breathe through chaos, how to lean into patience, how to listen beyond words.

Be steady. Be wise. Don't react rashly.

She wanted to be that woman, the one unaffected by circumstance, anchored regardless of the storms raging around her. But this? This was a major test.

Even with all her emotional and spiritual intelligence, even with decades of training her brain and taming her emotions to rise above conditions, this betrayal seared her to the bone. The worst part wasn't just the pain. It was the sheer waste of it all. They should be laughing together, thriving in this chapter of life, enjoying simple mornings, sunsets, shared stories, even without the wealth they'd once had. Rich in time, in companionship, in peace. Instead, here they were. Wounded. Fractured. Standing amid the ruins, she had long warned about. Michele had predicted it. She had told Nick, over and over, that his downward spiral, his anger, his despair would only magnetize more destruction. The law of attraction wasn't a theory. It was physics.

He couldn't save himself, and she couldn't save him either. Now, they stood on the precipice of a reality neither of them wanted and one they could ill afford. Financially, a divorce would devastate them both. Their house, her glorious home, would be sold and the funds divided. They would each go their separate ways into a world that had no patience for the aging.

Ageism was alive and well. It was one of the few "isms" still accepted without challenge. Anyone over forty was considered old in today's world. In their "later" years, Nick and Michele couldn't expect to have the welcome mat rolled out. The loneliness, the isolation… she knew the statistics. She knew the real costs and the emotional toll.

Research was clear. Grief from divorce could take up to four years to even begin to dissipate. Some people never recovered. Bitterness calcified their hearts for decades. Then there was the toll on the body—the shortened lifespan, the increased mental health struggles, the loneliness that clung especially hard to divorced men. She'd seen it firsthand. But more than the pragmatic, cold calculus of divorce, there was still love. Despite what he had done—the lying, the betrayal—deep inside Nick, there was a light that had once illuminated her world. A soul that had touched hers so profoundly, so unmistakably, that even now, she could feel it flickering through the darkness. It was faint, shadowed by pain and mistakes. But it was still there.

Michele watched him now, standing awkwardly beside the half-packed suitcase, waiting, unsure whether to stay or go, unsure whether hope still had a place. There was something in his face she hadn't seen in a long time. A lightness. A boyishness. A hope. His remorse didn't feel like a performance. It felt real.

Forgiveness is the fragrance the violet sheds on the heel that has crushed it.

Mark Twain's words floated up from the edges of her consciousness. She certainly felt crushed, flattened under the weight of betrayal, of broken promises and lies. Could she be the violet? Could she be the one who, even when trampled, released grace instead of bitterness? She didn't know yet. But Michele knew one thing for certain: her prime objective had always been to live more fully as her true self. To choose love over fear. Wisdom over victimhood. Light over darkness. Standing here, bruised and trampled, she recognized that this was another opportunity to fulfill that sacred commitment. Another chance to become who she was meant to be.

"Okay, Nick. You don't have to leave. Not yet. Not now." The words spilled out of Michele's mouth before her mind had a chance to catch up. They surprised her as much as they stunned Nick. His face lit up, equal parts delight and disbelief, as if he were a condemned man handed a sudden stay of execution.

He stepped forward, arms outstretched, heart wide open. "Thank you. Thank you!"

Michele instinctively backed away, raising both hands like a traffic cop. "No. No. No." Her voice was sharp, commanding.

Nick froze mid-step, his arms dropping to his sides like broken wings. He backpedalled quickly, hands up in surrender. "Sorry. Too soon. I get it."

She inhaled, steadying herself, holding on to the thread of calm she had so fiercely reclaimed. Keeping a deliberate, necessary distance between them, Michele spoke again, her voice clear and strong. "There will need to be changes around here—new conditions. If you can comply, if I feel the energy shift, and only if I believe there's a real future for us, then we can move forward. But it's going to be one day at a time. Agreed?"

Nick nodded hard and fast. "Agreed!" His voice sounded thick with gratitude and desperation.

"Good!" Michele gave one final curt nod. Turning on her heel, she left the room without looking back. Inside, the battle raged on, the voice that loved him, the voice that doubted, the voice that demanded self-respect. But she knew this: nothing would be gained by standing still in fear.

Could she do it?

Could he?

Could they save their marriage, rebuild trust, and find the love that once burned so brightly between them?

There was only one way to find out.

Just do it.

CHAPTER EIGHT

Since Michele had permitted him to stay, Nick felt as if he'd been enlisted in some brutal secret service training program—one designed to break you down before building you back up. Every day was a mission. Every hour a test of endurance. Some mornings, he had to scale back from the lowest depths of disgust with himself just to greet Michele with a genuine smile. He forced himself to give thanks for the blessings in his life, though, given the current circumstances, this proved challenging. Making Michele's coffee with care and listening to her plans and dreams without letting his inner storm hijack the moment tested his focus a little less. Other times, he barely dodged the emotional grenades she hurled his way. Hate bombs, he called them privately. They came without warning, explosions of rage and heartbreak when the memories of his betrayal tore through her composure. Then came the litany—question after question, each one peeling back another layer of guilt.

What had he done with Joanna?
How often?
What had he felt?
Had he ever loved her?
Had he intended to leave Michele for her?

So many questions. So much pain. Not just for Michele, but for him, too. She dug for the truth like an archaeologist, relentless in her search for the origins of the ruin they now lived in. She would not stop until she unearthed every fragment. And Nick? He took it. Every. Shovel. Full. Because this was his atonement. He had promised the truth, no matter how ugly, no matter how difficult, and he would keep that promise if it killed him. Sometimes, the truth seemed to soothe her, like an antiseptic sting that signalled healing had begun. Other times, it set her ablaze with fresh fury, and neither of them could pacify the inferno.

But as the days turned into weeks, the worst of the dust settled. Michele's unpredictability softened, like a storm losing strength as it moved out to sea. The marriage counselling helped. Not because the counsellor told them anything Michele hadn't already tried to tell him a thousand times, but because it gave them a neutral field, a referee, someone who sat silently and let the truth land without bias. Strangely, it was after those sessions that the real healing flickered to life.

Every week, they went to lunch afterward at one of their previously favourite restaurants. No grumbling over prices, Nick had made a vow to stop worshipping at the altar of money, and for once, he honoured it. At lunch, they laughed, they teased, they reminisced. Sometimes it felt like stepping into a time machine, back to the days when they were just two people in love, no titles, no businesses, no betrayals. Nick's heart ached with simultaneous love and guilt. He had nearly lost her. And for what?

Even amidst the wreckage, these small moments acted like a balm, soothing the open wounds, stitching something fragile but precious back together, hour by hour. Of course, it wasn't all soft landings. Some days, the house still became a battlefield. Michele would glare at him across the room, arms flailing wildly, and unload her righteous fury. Nick would stand there and take it—no defence, no offence—just as he had promised. He knew the only way to rebuild trust was simple in theory and brutal in practice.

Never break another promise again.
Tell the truth, even when it hurts.
Show up, even when it shamed him to do so.
One day at a time.

As part of his commitment, Nick agreed to get clinical help. It was a bitter pill. He, Nick Stavros, who used to laugh at people who claimed they had "anxiety," now wore the diagnosis himself. Anxiety. The word felt foreign, insulting, humiliating. He was too proud. Too tough. Too Greek to admit to something like that. Or so he thought. But strangely, once it was named, he felt relief. It wasn't weakness. It wasn't failure. It was a signpost. A signal that he had fallen but could still rise.

He hated labels, but this one gave him something he hadn't had in a long time: a direction to aim for. A new hill to climb and aim higher was exactly what Nick Stavros decided to do.

* * *

THE END OF another day descended, and the twilight slipped gently around them, bathing the room in soft gold.

"I've decided to investigate driving an Uber," said Nick, as he and Michele sat together in a peaceful moment. He kept his tone casual, but inside, he was tight with anticipation. "You've been saying I needed to find a purpose. Something to get me out of the house. Something to make some money." He waited, heart hammering quietly beneath his ribcage.

Michele said nothing for a moment, simply tilted her head, one eyebrow arched.

Nick rushed to fill the space. "I don't want us to start another business. No staff. No big stress. I just want to do something where I'm in control. Simple. Manageable." He took a breath. "It won't bring in much money, but it'll tide us over for now." He glanced at her, searching her face for a verdict. "What do you think?"

Michele's lips curved into a genuine, delighted smile. "I think it's a wonderful idea," she said. "You get to be your own boss. Set your own hours. And it gets you out into the world again. Meeting people. Ordinary everyday people with their own lives and problems."

The tension in Nick's chest released in a long, quiet sigh of relief. He hadn't realised how much he craved her encouragement. How much he still hungered for her approval and belief in him. He nodded, feeling a flicker of energy sparking to life inside him. Something he hadn't felt in a long time.

"I've already looked into it," he said, sitting forward now, a new charge of momentum in his voice. "Startup costs are manageable—some paperwork and background checks. I can rent a car to begin with. I've run the numbers, and it's enough to keep us going for now."

As Nick laid out his preliminary plans, insurance, peak driving hours, earning estimates, and registration requirements, he felt something surprising stir inside him. A sensation he hadn't tasted since the days when every deal he touched seemed to turn to gold. His old Midas touch. But this time, it wasn't gilded with the rush of ego. It was steadier. Quieter. There was a new thread woven into it. Humility. No flashy empire. No accoutrements. No status. Just the calm dignity of a man willing to start over.

Nick smiled, not the brittle, forced smiles he'd worn like armour in months past, but a real one. Driving an Uber might not seem like much to the outside world. But to him, it was a beginning. For the first time in longer than he could remember, Nick felt something priceless ignite within him—respect for himself.

* * *

Letting Nick stay seemed to be working. Every day, Michele saw him becoming more aware, more conscious, more deliberate in his decisions and his words. His actions now spoke louder than any promise ever could. He did everything he said he would. He attended to her needs without her having to ask. He listened, really listened. He talked when talking was needed, stayed silent when silence was sacred. He showed up at the marriage counsellor's office, week after week, owning his mess without excuse. He met with his psychologist, faced his demons, read every resource, practised his meditations, and took every recommendation seriously. And now, with his talk of becoming a rideshare driver, Nick showed something deeper than just repentance. He showed a willingness to protect and provide, not with grandeur, not with ego, but with quiet commitment. He was honouring his promise: *Whatever it takes.* It was everything she had wished for. She only hoped it wasn't too little, too late. Michele breathed out slowly, letting the thought pass without grabbing onto it.

Even though she had chosen to give him and their marriage a second chance, she was still startled sometimes by the depth of rage that lived inside her. She had forgiven him, but she had not forgotten. Her body, her mind, and her emotions reminded her often of the trauma. That sinister voice would creep in at the edges of her consciousness, whispering things she didn't want to hear.

Fool me once, and it's your fault. Fool me twice, and it's my fault for taking you back.

Was she a fool for giving Nick another chance? Some days, she wasn't sure. Her emotions would drive her around the corners of her mind at breakneck speed, swerving, crashing, destroying her hard-won equilibrium. One moment, she was kind, gentle, even loving toward him. The next, she was a fury—accusing, raging, a tempest of pain he could neither escape nor fix. Like a madwoman reliving the violation again and again, she would hurl herself back into the hurt, reigniting the fire within herself.

Yet there was nothing for it but to hold on. Hold on to faith. Faith in herself. Faith in the higher consciousness that had never betrayed her. Faith in her inner being that remained untouched, unshaken, no matter what storm battered the surface. She gripped that faith with both hands, waiting for the rogue waves of emotion to pass like a ship in the night. When they did, when calm waters returned, Michele reminded herself that even with all the chaos, she was still putting one foot in front of the other.

The joy was in the journey…

CHAPTER NINE

Nick woke before the summer sun even crested the horizon, the sky still heavy with night. A restless energy buzzed under his skin, part anticipation, part trepidation. He dressed quietly, collected the lunch Michele had packed the night before—a small act of love that hadn't gone unnoticed—and slipped into his leased car, setting off for his first rideshare job. Never, in his wildest imaginings, had he pictured this: Seventy years old. Once a man who signed multi-million-dollar contracts, now behind the wheel, carting strangers around the suburbs like a glorified lackey.

"Not the way I expected to spend my retirement," he muttered, following the pulsing line on the Uber map. "But it is what it is. Time to toughen up and make the most of it."

As he navigated the winding, darkened streets of the estate, he squinted at half-hidden house numbers. *Mental note*: Buy a decent torch. It was the first of many mental notes he would make today. He nearly missed his first fare if not for the flash of white—a young woman in a barely-there dress, waving frantically in his headlights. Nick slowed to a stop. She yanked open the passenger door, poking her pretty, too-young face inside.

"Nick?"

"Yes. Vanessa?"

"That's me." She slid into the front seat, her dress riding even higher up her thighs, and slammed the door shut without ceremony.

Nick figured she was maybe twenty at best. She smelled, unmistakably, of recent sex. He craned his neck instinctively toward the footpath, spotting a lanky, awkward boy standing there, watching her leave with a mix of hope and heartbreak.

"What about him?" Nick asked, jerking his chin toward the kid. "Is he coming too?"

"Fuck no." Vanessa rolled her eyes dramatically. "I only met him tonight." She crossed her legs defiantly, a silent verdict on her night's escapades.

Nick suppressed a smirk. *Times don't change much... just the language.*

He gestured forward. "Can I do a U-turn further down, or is there a quicker way out?"

"Fuck, man, I don't know." Vanessa tossed a withering glare out the window toward her abandoned conquest. "I've never been here before, and I'm not coming back."

Nick chuckled under his breath and set off, careful to keep the ride smooth and quiet. "Music okay? Air-con all right?" he asked, adopting his best professional tone.

Vanessa barely nodded, already pulling out her phone. Her thumbs attacked the screen with the ferocity of a boxer, message after furious message.

Nick figured she was probably posting live updates to her friends about how terrible her one-night stand had been. He kept his eyes on the road and his mouth shut.

Rule number one: No unnecessary conversation.

Rule number two: Let the passenger lead, if they want to talk.

Rule number three: Make it more than a ride. Make it an experience.

If he were going to do this, he would be the best. It was what he had always done. No matter the job. No matter the status. His expectations of himself were higher than anyone else.

Fifteen minutes later, Nick pulled up to another nondescript private address. "We're here," he said.

Vanessa barely looked up from her phone. Then she blinked, scanned the unfamiliar surroundings, and finally smiled. "Thanks, Nick. I wish my date had been as caring as you." She flashed him a bright grin and slid out of the car. "See ya!" she called and disappeared into the shadows just as the first hints of dawn began to lift the darkness.

Nick watched her go, shook his head once, then tapped to accept another fare. He glanced up into the rear-view mirror, and this time, he grinned at his own reflection, uttering his verdict on his first foray into being an Uber driver. "Not so bad."

He paused, checking his next pickup. Vanessa reminded him of his younger years, the footloose freedom, the casual chaos of late nights and early mornings. The life of the young, still convinced they had forever ahead of them.

They don't know, he thought, *they just don't know how short this time is.*

He straightened in his seat, feeling the familiar tightening of purpose in his chest. "Not for me," he said aloud, with quiet conviction. "I'm married to the best woman in the world. And I intend to keep it that way."

A huge smile stretched across Nick's face as he set off to his next fare, the first rays of sunrise painting the road ahead in gold. With each kilometre, he realised there was more to this job than just navigating streets and collecting fares. The real navigation was through people—their stories, their moods, and, as he was about to discover, their smells. When it came to rideshare driving, your nose could reveal almost as much as your eyes. Michele had often explained how the olfactory sense was the strongest of the five senses, the one capable of stirring vivid memories from the past with just one fleeting sniff. That was the secret weapon of perfume and pheromones: chemical signals transmitted like an invisible language, whispering things no words ever could.

Like Vanessa, he thought, *reeking of fresh sex.*

And now, his next fare. Nick wound down the passenger window as he pulled up next to a scruffy-looking man in his thirties standing outside a 7-11 store, a single plastic grocery bag swinging from his hand.

"Jake?"

The man nodded, his wild eyes darting nervously, hair clinging damply to his forehead.

Nick braced himself as Jake climbed into the front seat and was immediately assaulted by a thick cloud of incense and stale perspiration. *Jesus, Mary, and Joseph,* Nick thought, choking back a cough. *I'm going to have to fumigate the car after this one.* He eased into traffic, heading for the destination listed in the app: a local church. *Well,* Nick thought, *that explains the incense. Doesn't explain the BO, though.*

Before he could even ask if the music and air conditioning were okay, Jake started mumbling. Low at first. Then louder. Faster. Unintelligible.

Nick threw him a sideways glance. "You okay, mate?" he asked, unsure if he wanted an answer.

Jake's head snapped toward him so fast, Nick half-expected it to keep spinning, *Regan-style* from *The Exorcist.*

Dear Lord, Nick thought, *he's speaking in tongues.*

Papou had told Nick old Bible stories about people overtaken by the Holy Spirit, babbling in ancient, unknown languages. Nick had always chalked it up to folklore. Apparently not.

Jake's mumbling turned into preaching. Loud, impassioned proclamations about the end of the world, the coming of the Lamb, and the wrath of Revelation. As the fervour built, so did the smell. Jake sweated through his shirt like a farm animal under a heat lamp. Nick, trying to be subtle, turned the air-conditioning down another few degrees and cracked his own window. All he wanted now was to get the guy to the church where a priest, preferably armed with holy water, could take over. He checked his app for traffic updates and cursed under his breath. Breakdown ahead.

Of course.

Jake's eyes gleamed feverishly. "Do you believe in God?" he demanded.

Nick gripped the wheel a little tighter. "Yes."

Jake leaned closer. "Which God?" His voice turned sharp, almost threatening, as if the wrong answer might earn Nick a ticket straight to hell.

Nick didn't hesitate. "I'm Greek Orthodox," he said, praying to every saint he could think of that this would pass muster.

Jake's face broke into a sudden, beatific smile. "Good. A Christian." He lifted both hands skyward and resumed speaking in tongues with renewed vigour.

Nick kept his eyes trained on the road, murmuring his own silent prayers: *Deliver us from evil, O Lord, and get us to that damn church.*

Despite the madness swirling in his passenger seat, Nick found himself strangely amused and weirdly enlightened. In just a few hours, his carefully built ideas about people were being dismantled one bizarre encounter at a time.

Michele had been right all along. He'd been living in an echo chamber. His own world of woes and his own bullshit playing on repeat. He'd had no real idea what was happening in the streets just outside his door—until now.

His spirits lifted as he dropped Jake off, watching with some relief as the man staggered up the church steps, arms still flailing toward the heavens. Nick chuckled, shook his head, and tapped "Complete Ride" on his app. He pulled back onto the main road, feeling a surprising lightness in his chest.

There was a whole world out here. Messy. Mad. Magical. And he was just getting started.

Let's see what other insights today's going to serve up, he thought, grinning to himself. He couldn't wait to find out.

The remainder of the day passed without incident. There were hospitality staff heading to early shifts, half-asleep but polite. Adults with suspended licences catching rides to work, sheepish but grateful. Then came the parade of women in athleisure wear, some off to lunch, others balancing grocery bags and toddlers, all wielding opinions, conversations, and life stories. One after another, they slid into his car. Strangers, but also fellow travellers in this strange, modern dance of movement and meaning. They talked about their jobs, their kids, and their frustrations. About lazy husbands, overbearing bosses, and sick parents. Some vented. Others just wanted to be heard. And they all thanked him, not just for the ride, but for the listening.

"You're not like other drivers," they said, again and again.

"They won't even help with your bags," one woman grumbled as Nick carefully lifted her suitcase into the trunk. "Some are downright rude."

Nick just smiled, nodded, and said nothing in return. He wasn't about to criticise his peers. He knew everyone was fighting their own invisible battles.

But inwardly, something swelled. Not arrogance. Not achievement. *Alignment.* There was something deeply satisfying in doing a simple job with excellence. With heart. With presence.

It became clear by mid-morning that, somehow, without fanfare or realisation, Nick had stepped into a rhythm, a role that fit. Not because it paid well. Hell, it paid below minimum wage. Not because of the status. There were no bragging rights attached to what he was doing. But because something in him was changing with every trip. He saw that his passengers were just like him—people who were trying to live better lives. Better fathers, better mothers. Better leaders. Better workers. Better humans. In the quiet moments between rides, Nick felt the stirrings of a deeper insight. He was becoming a better man. He wasn't just driving people around. He was being moved himself.

Hour after hour, Nick ferried people to and from their destinations, between chapters of their lives, between decisions and discoveries, between breakdowns and breakthroughs. Before he knew it, he'd hit close to the twelve-hour driving limit and enjoyed every minute of it. Except, of course, for when back-to-back rides left him regretting that second bottle of water without a toilet stop in sight. His bladder had survived, but only just.

As the sun dipped low, painting the sky in soft apricot light, Nick ended the day on a note of quiet contentment. He expected to feel exhausted. Instead, he felt invigorated. Not wired or buzzing, but alive. Not lost or uncertain, but aligned. That word pulsed through him like an anthem. He hadn't felt this way in years. *Alive and aligned.* Not since the early days of building his first company, when every move had been lit with purpose, had he felt like this. He felt like a traveller again on a path he didn't entirely recognise, but one that thrilled him with the promise of discovery. A solid hum ran through his body, like an engine finally firing after too long in the shed. He was back. Or at least, well on his way.

CHAPTER TEN

A s Nick found his footing, Michele lost her balance. The more he improved his attitude, his actions, and his genuine attention to his growth, the more the toxic chatter inside her intensified. She wanted to share in his delight at finding a new passion and purpose. She wanted to celebrate his aliveness and alignment. But at the same time, a darker urge clamped its cold hand around her throat. A desperate, bitter voice inside her whispered…

How can he just forget everything he did? Do my feelings and what he's done to me, to our marriage, mean so little that he can just move on?

Michele knew how unreasonable it was. She knew that dredging up the past only activated hate, not healing. She knew that every time she returned to it, she was choosing the wound over wellness. But reason didn't always win. Before she even realised it, she would find herself veering the conversation back, transmuting moments of potential love into icy gulfs of loathing. Until finally, one afternoon, the dam broke.

She turned on him. "I can't do this, Nick," she blurted, the words punching through the fragile peace between them. "I don't think this is going to work. I thought I could… but I just can't seem to get it out of my mind. Maybe it would be best if you moved out. For a while."

Nick stood there, silent. Not pleading. Not defending. Just crushed.

Michele saw it, the slump of his shoulders, the wounded confusion in his eyes, and still, some hardened, hurting part of her didn't stop. She fled before he could speak, retreating to the bedroom, locking the door behind her like a soldier fortifying a crumbling fortress. She didn't want to see him. She didn't want to unleash more cruelty with her words, words she once wielded like prayers and now flung like daggers. Throwing herself onto the bed, she buried her face into the pillow and sobbed. Sobs of rage, of grief, of sheer exhaustion racked her body.

She hated herself for being so cruel.

She hated Nick for being so cruel.

She hated life for being so damn cruel.

Not long ago, she had felt alive and aligned. Able to live from inspiration, to touch the higher vibrations of joy and creativity with ease. Her life had been abundant, rich in health, wealth, and happiness. Now she floundered at the bottom of the emotional scale, trapped in anger, blame, resentment, and grief. She was a prisoner caught in a tightening neural loop, like prey being slowly strangled by a boa constrictor. If she couldn't break free, she knew what would happen. It wouldn't be Nick who damned their marriage to failure. It would be her.

I have to find a way to move forward, she thought, pressing her tear-soaked cheek into the pillow. *I have to forgive and forget.*

Eventually, the sobs subsided, leaving only the aching silence. Michele rolled over, tucking the pillow under her head, and stared up at the ceiling.

I need to sleep, she told herself. *To recalibrate. To recentre. When I wake up, I'll know what to do.*

* * *

NICK SPENT THE night tossing and turning, wondering where it had all gone wrong. Everything had seemed to be going so well. They were laughing again. Talking easily. Building something new from the ashes. Then, out of nowhere, Michele had snapped and ordered him to move out. Again. The first time, he understood. This time, he was lost. He thought they were making progress. He knew he was.

Standing at the bathroom mirror, shaving with slow, careful strokes, he muttered to his reflection, "Must be tough for her. Not sure I could've done as well as she has if the shoe was on the other foot."

Deciding to take the morning off from Uber driving and stay close, Nick splashed on the aftershave Michele liked best, the one that always made her smile when she buried her face against his neck. He dressed and headed to the kitchen to prepare the coffee machine. The familiar hum of the grinder filled the space, comforting in its simplicity. He was just setting out two cups when Michele padded in, barefoot and red-eyed.

"Morning, darling," he said, offering her a tentative smile and a cautious step forward.

She lifted a hand slightly, not a push, not a slap, just a gentle signal. *Stay there.* "Morning," she said. Her voice was calm. No anger. No fire. Just something softer, heavier. "Can we talk?"

Nick's heart thudded. "Sure," he said, sliding onto a kitchen stool, ready for whatever came next.

Michele perched beside him, her hands twisting in her lap. "Sorry about flying off the handle yesterday," she began, but even though I've forgiven you for what you did, I've been having trouble forgetting it. It haunts me."

Nick stayed silent, studying her face as her frown deepened and her mouth tightened.

"I understand…" he began.

But she cut him off with a shake of her head. "No, you don't. You can't. It hasn't happened to you, so you can't possibly understand. And that's okay." She paused, drawing a steadying breath. "But neither could I. I couldn't understand why I'm fine one minute and a crazy woman the next. You've been doing everything you said you would. You've kept every single promise you made. And I am truly grateful for that."

Nick braced himself for the blow he felt sure was coming.

But Michele's voice softened. "And then, this morning, when I woke up, it hit me." She reached out, taking his hands in hers. "I had forgiven you. But I hadn't forgiven me."

Nick blinked, genuinely stunned. *Forgive herself? For what?* In his mind, she was the innocent. The angel who had saved them both from destruction. He was the guilty one. He was the sinner. What could she possibly need forgiveness for? "I don't understand," he said.

Michele gave a small, sad smile. "Nick, I've been punishing you. Relentlessly. Ruthlessly. I've been a total bitch."

"You had every right to be."

"No," she shook her head. "Not like this. Not for this long." Her eyes shimmered, but her voice stayed steady. "This has been going on for three months now. It's become a prison for both of us. It has to stop. I have to stop." She squeezed his hands. "What's done is done. I can't change it. Neither can you. If I keep clinging to the past, I'm just hurting both of us. I need to forgive myself for the part I played leading up to the affair, and for how long I've stayed stuck in being the victim ever since." She straightened, lifting her chin, her voice intensifying with obvious conviction. "I'm done!"

In that moment, Nick could have sworn he saw a shaft of light break through the kitchen window, bathing Michele's face in a soft, holy glow. She looked like the angel he had always suspected her to be.

"I want us to move on," she said. "Together." A smile lifted her face, chasing away the shadows.

"Oh, darling." Nick pulled her into his arms. "Me too. More than anything." He felt her soft laugh rumble against his chest.

"No more apologies," she said. "Time to start a new life. Attract more opportunities. Live with more joy, together."

"Agreed," Nick whispered, sealing the vow with a kiss to her forehead, holding her tight, feeling the first true peace he'd known in years wash over him. Right there, in that sun-washed kitchen, wrapped in each other's arms, Nick knew a new chapter had begun. Not perfect. Not easy. But possible, and sometimes, that was all one needed to write the story of a lifetime.

* * *

STANDING IN THE garage, Michele waved Nick goodbye as he backed out and set off for his next Uber shift. She stayed rooted to the spot as the door slowly descended, the mechanical hum giving way to stillness. Folding her arms gently across her chest, she stared at the closed door, then let her eyes slip shut. In that stillness, something shifted. It was subtle at first, like the soft breeze before a storm clears. Then came a sigh. And just like that, the energy around her lifted. It wasn't a dramatic flash or a spiritual epiphany, just a quiet, undeniable release. A sense of freedom unfolded inside her. Not the kind that comes from breaking chains, but the kind that comes from laying down a heavy burden one has carried for far too long. It wasn't freedom from Nick's betrayal. It was freedom to love again.

To heal. To live… fully.

This was the true power of forgiveness, not just forgiving Nick, but forgiving herself. Until she acknowledged the part she had played—the moments of withdrawal, the sharp-edged criticisms, the cold silences—until she could own her part in the unravelling, she and Nick would never fully recover. Now she did.

The greatest freedom we have is the freedom to choose what we focus on.

She had been focusing on the hurt. The betrayal. But now she was choosing the future, a brighter future liberated from the past. With that decision came clarity and renewed commitment. A future filled with health, wealth, and happiness. All the things Nick had once chased so desperately. But now, together, they might simply receive. It was never about striving, or fixing, or controlling. They had walked through their dark night of the soul, together, and somehow, against the odds, had come out the other side. It was about alignment and attraction with forgiveness as the doorway.

Such a simple equation, she thought.

Forgiveness → Freedom
Freedom + Focus + Feeling + Flow = A Fulfilling Future

With a contented smile, Michele turned and wandered back into their home, each step deliberate. She let her hand trail across the cool surface of the cabinet before pausing in the entryway to admire the light spilling through the glass sliding doors. This home wasn't just a house. It was their creation. It held their story. Now, it would cradle their rebirth. At the deepest level of her being, Michele knew she and Nick had been fundamentally changed, not just healed but transformed.

CHAPTER ELEVEN

"I TELL YOU, MATE, THIS has been the best fucking holiday we've had."

"Check it out," said another, tapping madly on his phone, then holding it up. "Bro, you've got five-star reviews coming outta your wazoo."

Nick chuckled. He'd been watching his Uber ratings steadily rise, and he was quietly chuffed. It was funny how a simple number could light up a part of him he thought had gone dark.

"This has gotta be the best Uber ride I've *ever* had," said the third, grinning ear to ear.

Nick cast a quick glance in the rear-view mirror at the merry trio. Three young Greek blokes in their twenties, crammed shoulder-to-shoulder across the back seat like kookaburras on a fence. They reminded him so much of his own sons, cheeky, intelligent, always one line away from a punchline.

"How long have you been doing this?" asked the one in the middle, clearly the ringleader. There was a gleam in his eye Nick recognised too well. That was him, once. Smart-mouthed, overconfident, always looking to stir things up just for the hell of it.

"Only a few months," said Nick, happy to chat.

"Money any good?"

Nick snorted. "Terrible." The honesty landed with a beat of laughter from the back seat. "But it's a means to an end," Nick added. "I made a promise to someone very important to me. I'm keeping it. Joyfully, even if sometimes I have to squeeze the joy through clenched teeth."

The one on the left, the phone guy raised an eyebrow, eyeing Nick's gold watch. "You don't look like someone who has to drive for Uber."

Nick smiled, glancing at them in the mirror. "Long story." Wry smirk. End of subject.

"Got any kids?" the ringleader asked.

"Three boys," Nick replied. "You three remind me of them... a lot." His voice softened. Being around young people was like a tonic; one he didn't realise he'd missed until now. There was something about their unfiltered energy, their blind optimism. It lit something inside him. The car fell into a natural rhythm of conversation, Nick talking about his sons, them talking about their jobs, their travels, their lives.

Then the quieter one, who'd barely said a word, leaned forward. "Nick, I'm getting married at the end of the year. Any advice?"

Nick didn't hesitate. "Do you love her? Really love her?"

"Of course. I wouldn't be marrying her if I didn't."

"Not true," Nick said gently. "You could be marrying her because she'll make a great mother. Or because it's what's expected. Or because she wants to. There are a million reasons to get married. Love's only one of them."

The lads went quiet. The leader raised his eyebrows. The phone guy nodded slowly. They were listening now.

The quiet one considered for a moment, then said, "Nope. I love her. Really love her."

"Good. Then here's my advice," Nick said. "Never lie. Never cheat. Always tell the truth, even when it's hard." He paused for effect. "The truth will set you free. That saying has withstood the test of time for a reason."

A beat.

"You mean, tell her that her bum looks fat in those jeans?" the leader quipped, elbowing his mate. Laughter exploded in the back seat.

"Yes!" said Nick, raising his voice just above the racket. "Exactly!"

Three faces stared back at him, wide-eyed.

Nick could hear their inner monologues loud and clear:

You've gotta be kidding.

No woman wants to hear that.

That's a suicide mission. Certain death.

They started talking over each other, mock protesting his wisdom.

Nick held up a hand, laughing with them. "Alright, alright. Don't say it like that. Say she looks even better in that pink dress she wore last week. Or those blue pants you love. Tell the truth… gently, in a kind way."

A pause. Then a chorus of "ahhs" and "oohs" and "smart" rose from the back.

"That way," Nick continued, "you get in the habit of telling the truth. All. The. Time. It becomes second nature. Then lying becomes uncomfortable. You won't want to do it. That's how you build trust. That's how you keep your marriage alive. Aligned."

"Shit," the ringleader muttered. "I never thought of it like that. How'd you get so smart, mate?"

Nick met their eyes in the mirror, his smile tinged with depth. "The hard way," he said, winking. "And I have a wife who taught me most of it." He let that hang for a moment. Then added, "One more thing, boys—never forget: Happy wife, happy life."

They laughed together, the kind of laugh that melts the age gap into nothing.

When they pulled up at the airport, Nick jumped out to help with the bags. To his surprise, each of them hugged him. Not a polite one, but real, firm, heartfelt.

"Thanks, Nick. Not just for the lift, but you know," said the quiet one, eyes shining with sincerity.

Nick nodded. "My pleasure. Safe flight."

As they disappeared into the terminal, still laughing and ribbing each other, Nick stood for a moment beside the car. The breeze was light. The morning sun warmed his shoulders. He looked up, smiled, and whispered to himself, "Yeah. Now I get it. This is wealth. Not the kind you bank. But the kind you become."

On the way to his next pick-up, Nick found the traffic steadily building. Cars whizzed through roundabouts and intersections like racehorses out of the gate. It was late Friday afternoon, knock-off time, and everyone was in a mad dash to get home, cutting corners, zipping between lanes, and trying to beat the lights.

Ever the defensive driver, Nick eased back, extra cautious. No fare was worth a wreck. As he crept forward at the intersection, a cyclist shot out from behind a passing SUV and smashed straight into the front left of Nick's car. The impact sent the rider flying across the bonnet, hitting the asphalt with a sickening thud.

"Fuck!" Nick slammed on the brakes, heart jumping into his throat. He threw the door open and was at the cyclist's side in seconds. "Are you okay?" he asked, voice tight with panic.

The young man lay stunned, blinking up at the sky, shaking his head.

"Stay there. I'm calling an ambulance." Nick moved quickly. He knew the protocols. Ambulance, police, and a calm head. But as he tapped in the number, adrenaline took over. His hands trembled. His breath came too fast. This wasn't just a near-miss. This was an accident. By the time he returned, the cyclist was upright and inspecting the mangled remains of his carbon fibre bike.

"I didn't see you," Nick said. "You came out so fast from behind that car…"

"That's okay, man," said the rider, brushing dust off his elbow. "I was doing time trials for my big race next weekend."

Time trials? In peak hour traffic? Nick bit back the urge to snap. *Jesus. Some people are too dumb to be alive.*

"Listen. I'm okay. Had worse falls than that," the young man continued. "I called my dad. He's on his way. But fuck… look at it." He cradled the warped frame like a dead pet, visibly crushed.

Nick didn't respond. He was fighting his own shock now. His chest thudded. His palms were clammy. His stomach twisted with dread. With trembling fingers, he pulled out a cigarette and took a long drag. In over five decades of driving, Nick had never had an accident. Not one. His spotless record was a source of pride. Now it was smeared, maybe even shattered. And for what?

For a job that pays bugger all. For doing the right thing. For helping Michele. For playing the good guy.

His mind spiralled.

What the hell am I doing this for?

What's it going to cost to fix? What if they take this car off me?

What if I lose my Uber rating? What if I'm suspended? I've been busting my arse for weeks for pocket change… and this is the reward?

The bitterness rose quickly. The old Nick, the hard-edged, self-righteous, stressed-out businessman, started scratching at the door of his mind.

I didn't even do anything wrong.

The screech of tyres broke his thoughts. A sleek black SUV pulled up. A man in a polo shirt and boat shoes jumped out. "Hi, I'm Craig—Brad's father," he said, shaking

Nick's hand. "So sorry. I've told Brad a hundred times: no time trials on main roads." He shot a scathing look at his son. "Now your $20,000 bike is fucked. What the hell are you going to do next weekend for the big race? You think I can just buy you another one?"

Brad said nothing, clutching his broken handlebars like a toddler with a snapped toy.

Craig turned back to Nick; his voice lowered. "Let's exchange details. I'll wait for the cops and the ambulance. Just so you know, I'm happy to say this was Brad's fault… which it was." He glared at his son again. "Total stupidity."

As the two walked away, Nick watched Craig toss the bike into the boot like scrap metal.

He cares more about that bike than his son, Nick thought, incredulity curling in his gut.

Then he caught himself. Because wasn't he doing the same? Worrying about money before meaning. His first thought hadn't been: *Is the kid okay*? It had been: *How much is this going to cost me?*

He sighed and dragged again on his smoke. The fall from grace didn't need angels and lightning bolts, just a cracked bumper, a dented bonnet, and a side panel ding.

The police arrived first, followed by the ambulance. Because his helmet had been cracked, Brad was taken to hospital for scans, and true to form, his father drove off with the bike in the opposite direction.

Despite the full admission from both Brad and Craig, Nick wasn't in the clear.

"We're going to have to fine you, Nick," said the officer. "For not giving way at the intersection."

"What? It wasn't my fault," Nick snapped. "He literally came out of nowhere. You heard them. He said it was his fault."

"Doesn't matter. Even if a cyclist hits you, the law says you have to give way at a give-way sign. Trust me, you'd lose in court. You can fight it, but you'll pay court costs, too. Or we can just issue the fine now and be done."

The anger came fast. Hot. Sharp. Familiar. The authoritative, entitled, defensive tone in Nick's voice wasn't just angry, it was old. The tone of a man who used to think he was always right. The tone of a man who used to lie to his wife and justify it. Nick shut his eyes. Michele's words floated in, calm and clear:

"It's better to feel good than be right."

He breathed in. Out. Again. He wanted to argue. To fight. To win. But that man was not who he was anymore. Or at least, not who he wanted to be.

Nick nodded. "Okay, Officer. Write me the fine." *Obviously, the law supersedes common sense.*

When it was all over and the road cleared, Nick climbed back into his car. The fine sat on the passenger seat like a bad joke. He looked at it with a kind of tired detachment, then started the ignition and turned for home.

His first accident. His first fine other than speeding fines. His first brush with the old Nick in months. It stung. But it also illuminated something. The accident hadn't defeated him or his resolve. It had tested him. Maybe that was the whole point. Life didn't stop testing the moment one turned over a new leaf. If anything, it turned up the heat to see if the change would hold.

Michele would say this was an opportunity. A moment to recommit. To deepen his purpose. To choose peace over punishment.

Nick didn't know if he'd passed the test. But he hadn't failed it either. He'd stayed calm and told the truth. Owned his reaction. And let go. Somehow, as he drove home, even with the traffic fine mocking him from the passenger seat and his nerves still frayed, he felt something close to satisfaction. All things considered... he'd done alright.

CHAPTER TWELVE

"A LL THINGS CONSIDERED, IT TURNED out well," said Michele, after Nick recounted the cyclist accident in careful detail. "The kid could've been seriously hurt, and his father could've wanted to sue you every which way to Tuesday." She stepped forward and wrapped her arms around him.

Nick felt tense in her embrace, his body still carrying the echo of adrenaline, but she held him anyway. She knew the tension would ease. If given enough room, the trauma would leave his body in its own time.

"Why don't you go and have a cigarette?" she whispered. "Relax. Dinner won't be long."

He nodded and slipped out toward the summer house.

Michele smiled as he walked away. The tightness in him was unwinding, and for the first time in a long while, he looked lighter. More at ease in his skin. He wasn't smoking or drinking as much. Whether it was a conscious decision or the result of deeper energetic shifts, she wasn't sure. But she'd noticed. Either way, she was grateful that he seemed to be in brighter spirits and more in control of his inner demons. She'd never believed in the religious concept of good and evil, but living with Nick and witnessing his turmoil had renewed her appreciation for how the mind and emotions can play havoc, destroying hope, love, and faith.

Faith, she thought, sliding vegetables into the roasting tray. That's what had brought them here. Not blind hope. Not passive wishing, but unrelenting faith. She had carried it for both of them when Nick couldn't. Perhaps, in some unseen way, it had been enough. Enough to forgive, enough to rebuild, enough to call them both back to the truth of who they were.

She paused at the sink, hands motionless over the tap. She'd lived long enough to know that moments like these, where everything feels calm and almost whole again, were also when life tested you once more. Not cruelly, but truthfully. Tests of faith rarely arrived with fanfare. They crept in through the back door, innocuous at first, then unmistakable.

She'd seen it before. Just when you one starts to trust again, just when one begins to breathe, life asks, *So how are things really working out for you?*

Michele dried her hands and glanced through the window toward the summer house, where Nick stood under the fading sun, smoke curling around him like incense. He was different. That much she could feel. His energy had shifted. His choices were aligned. He was showing up every day with integrity, intention, and in brighter spirits.

But still, a tremor moved through her chest. Not fear. Not even doubt. Just... an instinct. She inhaled deeply. Their marriage had passed through fire, and that fire had forged something new. But embers can still burn with enough heat to reignite flames. Her face flushed with the sense that something else was coming. She didn't know why she felt it, but the sense was clear, unmistakable.

Her mind raced until it landed on an unexpected image. As much as she disliked physically violent sports, she saw two boxers slugging it out in a ring in her mind. Both were determined to win the mortal battle, knowing that only one of them would walk away victorious. It was a battle as much about wits and strategy as brute strength. Whatever the stakes, they were high because both men fought as if their lives depended on it, or perhaps their souls. Michele gasped and squeezed her eyes shut—hard. She didn't want to see anymore.

Turning back to her chopping board, she reopened them slowly, cautiously, wondering if an unseen intruder might appear in her kitchen, or worse, an unseen opponent might yet enter the ring of their marriage. Her heart sank. She hoped not, because she was unsure whether she possessed the moral fortitude to slug it out again. Giving herself a quick, fervent talking-to, she resumed chopping the broccoli, pledging to think only hopeful thoughts.

Nevertheless, she couldn't shake the whisper in the air...

Something is coming, and the next round is about to begin.

* * *

ONE MONTH TO the day, the unseen opponent appeared, lobbing into their lives like a heavyweight fighter, swinging with merciless precision.

"I can't fucking believe it!" Nick exploded in the kitchen. His voice ricocheted off the tiles. "Nothing. He fucking left me nothing."

Michele froze mid-step. She watched as Nick stormed the floor like a bull in an arena, arms flailing, jaw tight, fists punching the air in disbelief.

The invisible opponent was Nick's recently deceased father. The man who had promised him the family inheritance. The man who'd raised him with the expectation of legacy and loyalty. And in his final tyrannical act, he left it all, every last dollar, to Nick's younger brother.

"I helped him make that money!" Nick raged, voice cracking. "And now he's left it all to my no-hoper brother. Tens of millions of dollars and not one fucking cent to me!" The energy in the room roiled like a wild hurricane.

"Surely, you can contest it?" Michele offered gently, uncertain whether her suggestion would calm or provoke.

Nick spun on her. "We don't have the money to contest it. We're broke. Remember?"

It stung, not because of the words, but the tone, the sudden flick of blame in her direction. Michele's chest tightened. "Well, it's not my fault your father treated you like shit. I told you years ago, he was a narcissistic sociopath. This doesn't surprise me at all." She sat down hard at the table, breathing through the tension. *Here we go again,* she thought. The mood swings. The misplaced blame. The ghosts of old family wounds flung into the present like sharp-edged stones.

Nick's hands dropped to his sides. He looked as if he'd been sucker-punched. "Sorry. I didn't mean to take it out on you." He slumped into the chair beside her.

"I know. It's not fair." Michele softened, rubbing his back in slow circles. "But I know how betrayal feels."

She paused. Watched him. Let the words hang in the air.

Nick met her eyes. She could see the moment it clicked.

He nodded, the devastation in his expression shifting toward something more complex, recognition, perhaps. Or remorse.

"I know I betrayed you," he said. "But this is… this is even worse."

Michele blinked, startled. "Worse?"

"This is my father," he said, standing again, pacing now, unravelling. "What father does this to his eldest son? Leaves him nothing!"

The words hit her like a slap. She stood slowly, no longer feeling the urge to comfort. "You think this is worse than what you did to me?"

He stopped mid-stride.

"I don't say that to punish you," she continued, voice steady. "But betrayal is betrayal. You say your father cut you out of his life with a signature on a page. You cut me out with a lie and a choice. So don't talk to me about what's worse."

Nick looked down, and she couldn't tell if it was shame or controlled rage lurking inside him.

She sighed. Michele's anger dissipated as quickly as it had arrived. She could see how gutted he was. Not just because of the money, but because of what it meant. The rejection. The lack of recognition. The loss of identity.

"I get it," she said more gently. "I know what it's like to be dropped into a freefall of rage, confusion, and grief all at once. But you can't let it eat you alive."

Nick didn't answer. Instead, he stormed outside, the door slamming behind him like a final punctuation mark.

Michele stood alone in the quiet that followed, heart aching. She knew this pain, betrayal, guilt, rage, shame, and inadequacy. It came in layers, stacked high, until the weight of it felt unbearable. It was pressing down on Nick like it once had on her.

She could only hope that he would survive it. That he would not sink back into the darkness he'd only just clawed his way out of. Because betrayal, once endured, leaves a mark. When it arrives a second time, especially from family, it doesn't just cut—it severs!

CHAPTER THIRTEEN

THE ONLY THING KEEPING NICK sane was driving. Even when he was a young man, behind the wheel of his "pride and joy", usually the latest model Holden, something in him settled. He'd glide through the streets, windows down, music cranked, the road stretching out like an open invitation. Driving gave him an indescribable peace. It was the one place he could sit with his own thoughts, undisturbed. No expectations. No interruptions. Just him and the rhythm of the road.

He'd never called it meditation, not like Michele did, with her mat and her journal and her daily spiritual discipline, but it was the same thing in a different form. For Nick, the road was a sanctuary. Now, after the gut punch from his father's will, it was the only thing offering him comfort.

Every morning, before dawn's light brushed the horizon, Nick was on the road by 3:00 a.m., collecting his first fare of the day. Something about ferrying passengers in the stillness of early morning grounded him. He didn't have to think about his own problems when someone else was sitting beside him, sharing theirs.

He'd learned quickly that it wasn't the driving that liberated him. It was the people. Their stories. Their lives. Their quiet confessions that helped silence the angry voices in his head whispering vengeance, bitterness, and lack. Michele had always said healing often came disguised as the mundane. He now understood what she meant.

Unlike many other drivers who congregated at the airport holding bay to complain about Uber's commission, traffic, or politics, Nick kept his distance. The last thing he needed was more noise. He had had enough of that in his own mind. He chose solitude over cynicism and reflection over ranting. He worked alone, and he liked it that way.

He pulled up in front of a dilapidated block of six studio flats, headlights casting uneven shadows across the pavement.

"We won't be long. Mum's just bringing down the rest of the stuff," a teenage girl called out as she bounced up to the car with a tight ponytail and quick feet.

Nick got out to help. On the footpath was a small mountain of bulging plastic bags—clothing, pots, toys, and a haphazard assortment of household goods.

What the hell's going on here? he thought as he began stacking them into the boot, trying not to show his concern.

"Thanks," said a voice behind him.

He turned and involuntarily drew in a breath.

A woman, maybe mid-thirties, tried to offer him a polite smile despite the unmistakable bruises discolouring the side of her face. She moved carefully, with the residual stiffness of someone who had been struck too recently to forget.

"I just have to get the cat," she said. Then, turning to her children, "Come on, kids. Get in the car."

The girl took her younger brother's hand. "You get in, and I'll hand you Rupert."

Rupert? Nick squinted until he spotted the source: a tiny white mouse trembling in a plastic cage. Rupert—the pet mouse.

"Hold the cage steady," the girl instructed her brother like a little general, and Nick smiled despite himself.

"Yes, please," he added, eyeing the cage warily. The last thing he needed was rodent pellets across the upholstery.

The mother returned a moment later with a cat carrier, its occupant mewling softly, eyes wide and alert.

"All set," she announced as she slid into the front seat. Her tone was bright. Almost chipper. But her hands trembled in her lap.

Nick glanced at her, then at her children. She was doing everything in her power to keep it together. He checked the address on the app. "Highland Bay Supermarket? Is that right?"

She nodded. "Yes, that's right."

Odd place to go when you're carrying your whole life in jumbo bags, he thought, but didn't say it.

As they drove, the children whispered to each other in the back seat. The boy spoke softly to the mouse while his sister stared out the window, watching her old life fade behind them. It was clear now: they were homeless.

"We've been evicted," said the woman, her voice still bright. "But it'll be alright." She turned to face the back seat. "Won't it, kids?"

"Yes, Mum," they chimed.

"That's the spirit," said Nick, catching their eyes in the rear-view mirror. "Life has a strange way of working out in your favour if you believe it will."

The kids offered polite smiles, but Nick knew they weren't buying it.

Over the next half hour, the mother shared more, speaking in quiet tones as if she didn't want her children to hear. Though they surely already knew. Domestic violence. An abusive partner. An unpaid rent bill. A sudden disappearance. No money. No options.

Nick listened. That was all he could do. When he ran out of things to say, he listened harder. Eventually, they pulled into the supermarket car park.

"Just over there's fine," the mother said, gesturing toward a quiet corner by a loading dock.

Nick helped unload the bags while the children gathered their mouse and the mewling cat. Within minutes, they'd formed a small circle of belongings—an island of displaced survival.

"Are you going to be okay?" he asked, voice low.

"We'll be fine," she said, forcing a smile. "I'm going to call a friend who lives near here. I think we'll be able to stay with her for a few days."

Nick nodded, but he knew a lie when he heard one.

He leaned in so the children wouldn't hear. "Are you sure? I can take you to a halfway house. No charge."

Her eyes welled with tears. "Thank you. But truly, we'll be fine." She turned back to her children. "Doreen will come. She always does."

Nick didn't push. He nodded, offered a quiet farewell, and got back into his car.

As he drove off, the scent of cat fur and mouse cage lingered in the air, but it barely registered. What stuck with him was the image of those three souls—left behind in a supermarket car park with nowhere to go, pretending it was all going to be okay.

God, how lucky am I?

He turned onto the main road as the morning's heaviness melted into the warm flush of hope. One thought rose above the rest:

I cannot wait to get home. To hold Michele. To tell her that I love her deeply and without reserve. And mean every word.

* * *

BY LATE AFTERNOON, he pulled kerbside at a swank house in one of the elite suburbs. Out of the gate pranced three young men in full flamboyant flight. One wore a pink, fluffy tutu over glittering tights, wielding a wand crowned with a silver star. Another sported a flowing ruby-red velvet robe, a plastic gold crown perched atop his styled curls, and glitter smeared liberally across his cheekbones. The third? A vision in a white Grecian toga skirt, cinched just above the thigh, with oversized, bejewelled angel wings extending from his bronzed, bare back. All were bare-chested, oiled, and outrageously jacked—eight-pack abs carved from hours in the gym and possibly helped along by genetics or protein powder… or both.

Nick blinked. *Now this is going to be fun.*

The back door flew open with theatrical flair, and the toga-clad angel leaned in, batting long lashes over a golden gaze. "Are you Nick?"

"Yep. That's me," said Nick, a grin splitting his face as he soaked in the visual feast.

"Oh, fabulous! Boys, we've found our chariot!" the angel announced with delight. "Uber Cupid has arrived!"

They piled in, limbs flailing, giggling like schoolgirls on a champagne bender. "We're off to a Valentine's Day party," said the one in the crown, voice dripping with royal decree.

"But it's not February 14," said Nick as he pulled away from the curb.

"That's so boring of you, darling," sniffed the one in the tutu. "We celebrate love whenever we want. Love is always in season."

"Absolutely," chimed the Grecian angel. "Every day is Valentine's if you're fabulous enough."

"Well, in that case…" Nick punched through his playlist and hit play on Tina Charles' 1976 disco hit, "I Love to Love."

A high-pitched squeal erupted from the back seat. The wand waved, the crown tilted dramatically, and the toga flew dangerously high.

"Oh, my God, I love this song!"

"Turn it up, Nick! Louder!"

As the car filled with disco beats, the three of them bounced and bopped in the back seat like overexcited meerkats on MDMA. Nick quietly grooved in the front, drumming the steering wheel, basking in their uninhibited joy. It was impossible not to smile. Their energy was contagious, spilling out of them like laughter in a wind tunnel.

Gloria Gaynor, ABBA, Bee Gees, and Tina Turner followed in quick succession as Nick's playlist dipped into pop paradise.

Halfway through "Private Dancer," the angel leaned forward and purred, "Nick, you're a bit of a hair bear, honey."

Nick chuckled. "What's a hair bear?"

The car exploded in delighted squeals. "A hair bear," said the royal in the crown, clearly relishing his role as educator, "is an older, huggable, hairier man, preferably Greek. Like you."

Nick grinned into the rear-view mirror. "Sorry fellas, I'm a ladies' man. Always have been."

A collective groan echoed from the back.

"Oh, the Greek tragedy!" the angel wailed. "I thought Greek men swung both ways."

He crossed his legs with exaggerated flair and gave Nick the full *Basic Instinct* treatment.

Nick burst into laughter as he pulled to the kerb. "Here you go, fellas. Safe and sound for your Valentine's Day party."

"Thanks, Nick. Love to love you baby." The wand-wielding tutu dancer leaned forward and pecked him on the cheek.

"Bye, Nick," said the royal, likewise diving in for a quick peck.

"Here you go, babe," said the angel, leaning in with mock sultry eyes and placing a single red rose on the centre console. "Pity, you don't like men because I love hair bears." He leaned over to plant a lingering kiss on Nick's cheek.

Then they were gone in a wave of glitter and more giggles.

Nick watched as they pranced up the path toward the mansion with the last rays of sunlight dancing across their sequins and wings. He shook his head and chuckled. *Oh, to be young and unashamedly reckless.* Then, lifting the rose to his nose, he smiled and whispered to the empty car, "Give me a woman any day."

He tapped the app and queued up his next fare, disco still humming in the background.

CHAPTER FOURTEEN

T HE LAST FEW WEEKS, GRAPPLING with the sting of his father's betrayal and the echo of his own betrayal of Michele, had cracked something open inside Nick. His perspective had shifted. He no longer saw himself as the centre of the universe. He was beginning to realise that life wasn't just about accumulating wealth or proving a point. It was about something deeper, richer.

Strangely, despite earning less than minimum wage and working twelve-hour days, six days a week, he was happy. He felt useful. Aligned. Alive. Each morning, as the city still slumbered and the world wore its hush, he slipped behind the wheel and returned to what had always brought him peace: the road. The rhythm of movement, the silence between destinations, and now, the voices of his passengers—their confessions, their heartbreak, their small joys—each offering a window into the human condition. He was no longer just a driver. He was a witness. A conduit. And something in that mattered.

His five-star reviews were growing into the hundreds now. Passengers voiced compliments ranging from the expected to the deeply touching: *"Best Uber I've ever had"*, *"Why can't all drivers be like you?"*, and *"I needed that talk more than I knew"*. Unwittingly, Nick had become a sort of confidante on wheels, an outsider who offered sanctuary in the back seat of his car.

Through their stories, tales of love lost, of dreams deferred, of resilience forged in quiet suffering, Nick was rediscovering his own humanity. With every ride, his ego softened. His gratitude deepened. He was no longer chasing wealth. He was chasing wholeness.

He and Michele were stronger now, too, anchored by her unrelenting faith and his determination to honour every promise he'd made. Not always gracefully, but with steady, daily integrity. The kind that rebuilds trust with simple things like coffee on Sunday mornings, honest conversation, and walks in nature. Though he no longer had the millions he'd once been promised or the position of power he used to have, he had something better. Meaning. He knew now that true wealth wasn't measured in bank balances or bragging rights, but in the richness of one's character, the quality of one's connection, and the peace of knowing you're exactly where you're meant to be.

He had finally stopped asking, *"What's in this for me?"* and started wondering, *"How can I serve?"* That, more than anything else, had changed everything.

* * *

"So, WHAT DO you think?" Nick asked, swirling his coffee as they sat together in the morning sun. The garden shimmered with late summer light, and for the first time in weeks, the air between them felt easy, like a shared breath.

Michele tilted her head, considering his proposal. He had just outlined his plan to buy a car rather than continue renting. It was a significant shift and one that would eat into a substantial portion of their savings.

"I'm not against the idea," she said. "As long as we can afford it and it won't cut into our last reserves too much."

Nick nodded, already anticipating the follow-up. "We'd save hundreds a week, which means there's more left after Uber takes their commission to cover our personal expenses."

"So, this means you're committed to driving for a few years?" she asked.

"Yes, I'm in this for the long haul. Driving full-time for the next few years, at least." He paused and studied her face. "I know it's not what you or I envisioned retirement would look like. But I'm not doing it out of desperation anymore. I actually want this."

That was true. Somewhere along the line, the rideshare gig had transformed from a fallback plan into a mission. Each passenger, each conversation, each review was a step further from the man he used to be.

Michele looked at him. "And the shares?" she asked. "You've stopped counting on them."

Nick exhaled and gave a rueful half-laugh. "Yep. And if they come through, great. If not, this car, this work, it'll be enough until we decide on something else."

Michele lifted her cup and clinked it to his. "All right then. I'm in. You keep driving, and let's keep moving forward."

A surge of gratitude welled in Nick's chest, unspoken but palpable. Her trust still floored him. It wasn't just the money. It was the fact that she believed in him. Again. Still.

"I want to go all in," he said, riding the wave of momentum. "Make it easier for the passengers to spot me. I want to get a personalised plate: **UBER4U**."

Michele blinked. "Great idea, but how much is that going to cost? Personalised plates aren't cheap."

"Two and a half grand."

Her eyes widened. "Over two thousand dollars for a number plate? Can we afford it?"

"I know, it's a lot. But if I'm going to build something real, something that feels like more than just picking people up and dropping them off, I have to play a bigger game. This is about branding and my commitment for the future." Nick leaned forward, hope and conviction twining in his voice. "You and I, we've never played small, darling. Not in life. Not in business. Not even in love."

Michele stared at him, the corner of her mouth lifting. "Fine," she said. "Go all in, Nick. I know you'll make it work."

He beamed, emotion catching at his throat as he reached over and pulled her into a tight hug. For a long moment, they sat in that embrace, two people no longer rebuilding the past, but creating the future, one ride at a time.

* * *

THAT EVENING, AS Nick pulled out of the garage for an extra shift, Michele stood in the doorway, barefoot and contemplative, watching him go. He gave her a proud, beaming grin, and she waved him off with an ease she hadn't known in months.

"He's on a mission from God," she muttered with a soft smile, recalling the old Blues Brothers line. For the first time in a long while, the quip didn't land with irony; it felt true. He *was* on a mission. Not one given by Hollywood or heaven, perhaps, but something just as sacred. Something he'd given himself.

She turned back into the house, her fingers trailing along the door frame. Over these past few months, Michele had watched with the quiet intensity of someone who had everything to lose. She'd waited, not to test him, but to witness whether the man she once knew could find his way back not just to her, but to himself.

He had.

Not in one sweeping gesture. Not in grand confessions or perfect days. But in the small, consistent acts. The truth told, no matter how awkward. The Uber shifts logged without complaint. The choice to see a psychologist. That, perhaps, surprised her the most. Nick had always resisted therapy, dismissed it as unnecessary or indulgent. But this time, his resistance didn't stop him. This time, his trademark stubbornness, the same mule-headed drive that once exhausted her, was the very thing that saved him.

He had weaponised his willpower for growth instead of defence.

To be honest, Michele was a little in awe of it. Not just of his turnaround but of the grace with which he carried it. He wasn't just returning to the man she married. He was evolving into something more. Someone softer, yet stronger. Humble, yet still filled with that familiar fire. He found joy in the little things now. In music. In quiet moments. In the hilarious stories he brought home from his shifts.

Most of all, he carried a different energy, a lighter, steadier rhythm. A vibration that wasn't knocked around by every bump in the road, and that was the real miracle.

Because for Michele, the betrayal still flared on some days. There were unpredictable, painful hours when memory struck without warning, and she had to sit with the sharp ache of everything they'd almost lost. But even in those moments, there was something else. Something more powerful.

Gratitude that they hadn't given up when they easily could have. When it would've been simpler to separate and blame, and start over elsewhere. But they had chosen to stay, to fight, to heal. Together. That was no small feat. That was a victory. One of many couples never reached.

Now, as the next chapter of their lives quietly opened, Michele could feel something shifting in her bones. It didn't feel like surviving anymore. It felt like thriving.

CHAPTER FIFTEEN

"H EY, MATE, NEAT NUMBER PLATE," said the scruffy-looking guy in his twenties, nodding at the bold blue plate gleaming on the bumper—**UBER4U**—before flopping into the passenger seat of Nick's new Haval.

Nick flashed a grin. "Thanks. Had to do something to stand out in the crowd."

It had been Michele's idea to go Greek blue with the paint. "Easier to spot, and it suits your heritage," she'd said.

Between that and the cheeky custom plate, the car had become something of a local icon. Nick had embraced the new vibe completely, stocking his wardrobe with brightly coloured floral shirts that matched the car's cheerful energy. It started as a bit of fun, but soon the passengers began commenting. "Love the shirt", "Where'd you get it?" and Nick would beam like a peacock. Somehow, it all worked: the shirts, the car, the number plate. More than just a vehicle, the car had become both his new office and a symbol of the new life he was building. Every morning, while the rest of the world slept, he hit the road to meet new people, many of whom were lost souls seeking refuge from their troubles. Nick couldn't always spot them at first, but once the conversation started, it became clear. They were just another soul quietly asking for help, even if they didn't realise it themselves. For many, his car had become their sanctuary on wheels.

"We're off to the Chamberlain pub?" asked Nick, tapping the app.

"Yeah, that's right," the guy said, sinking deeper into the seat.

Nick pulled away from the kerb, easing into traffic. It took less than a block for the passenger to open up. He didn't even bother with pleasantries.

"You know, man… my life sucks."

Nick stifled a smile. He got this a lot. His car had become part therapist's couch, part confessional booth. If Michele had her meditations and journaling, this had become his own version of ministry. Helping others by simply listening. Sometimes offering a word. A nudge. And maybe, just maybe, giving someone what they didn't even realise they were looking for.

"Why's that?" Nick asked gently.

"It's women! I can't get a girlfriend. And when I do, I can't keep one."

Nick nodded, glancing sidelong at the guy. Baseball cap backwards, oversized tee, faded shorts that had seen better days, and a pair of thongs that had clearly walked many a regrettable mile.

"Well, where do you usually meet these women?" Nick asked.

"The local pub."

Nick raised an eyebrow. "And you dress like that?"

The guy shifted uncomfortably. "Yeah. I don't want 'em to think I've got money or nothin'."

Nick chuckled. "Mate, I don't think that's the problem."

The kid looked puzzled.

Nick sighed and steered into the teaching moment. "What do you do when you're at the pub?"

"Sit in the sports bar. Watch the footy. Horses sometimes."

"And you think that's where you'll find a quality woman?"

"Well, yeah. Where else would I go?"

Nick shook his head. "And when you meet one, what do you do?"

"I don't buy drinks. Most of 'em earn more than me anyway. If they're interested, they'll come over."

Nick couldn't help himself. He laughed. "Let me get this straight. You want a woman who drinks, won't expect you to pay for anything, and approaches you, while you're drinking beer and watching the footy?"

The guy blinked. "Yeah?"

"Okay. One more question. Do you smoke?"

"Yeah."

"Do you do drugs?"

"Sometimes."

"And you'll pay for that. But not a coffee or cocktail for someone you might actually build a relationship with?"

There was silence.

"Have you ever asked a woman out from work?"

"There's one I like, but she'll want me to pay."

Nick couldn't help it. "Good God, man. Shower. Shave. Buy a decent shirt. Get some cologne. Ask her out and pay for dinner."

"I don't have cologne. This car smells better than I do."

Nick told him the name of the aftershave he was wearing. "Buy it. Use it. Trust me. And when you're on a date, don't stare at your phone."

"What do I do then?"

"You talk to her. Ask her questions. What she likes. What she wants. What makes her laugh. You listen. That's what women want—attention, appreciation, and authenticity."

The kid was nodding now, leaning in.

"You want to know the secret to love?" Nick tilted his head toward him. "Put in the effort. Show up. Be kind. If you're lucky, find someone who lets you be you, but a better version of you."

Then, deciding to go all in, Nick asked, "You like sex?"

A startled pause. Then, "Yeah. Of course."

"When was the last time you had it?"

"Six months ago."

"Was it good?"

"Bloody oath it was. I had to pay $300 for it."

Nick raised his brows. "And yet you won't drop twenty bucks on a decent drink for a woman you might actually like?"

The penny finally dropped. The kid rubbed the back of his neck, suddenly sheepish. "I guess you're right."

"No guessing. I am right," said Nick with a grin as he pulled up outside the pub. "If you want different results, you've got to change your approach. Otherwise, you'll keep paying for prostitutes and complaining that love's a scam."

The guy opened the door, paused, and turned back. "Thanks, mate. You should run a workshop or something. You're like… an Uber Guru."

Nick laughed. "Cheers. Now go clean yourself up, Romeo. And don't forget the aftershave."

He watched as the guy shuffled toward the entrance, perhaps rethinking his entire approach to love, life, and laundry.

Punching the app, Nick set off for his next fare.

"Uber Guru," he mused aloud with a smirk. "Has a nice ring to it."

* * *

With her long, dark hair catching in the evening breeze, she stood beneath a streetlight on the corner, the golden glow clinging to her like honey. Her skirt barely covered anything, her cutaway top offered even less, and her stilettos, though dangerously high, carried her with the confidence of someone used to being watched. She looked young. Too young. Late teens, maybe early twenties at most. Nick slowed to a stop.

She slid into the front seat like she'd done it a hundred times. Turned toward him. Smiled. "Love the number plate," she said, her voice laced with sugar and secrets.

Nick chuckled politely. That line again. It had become a kind of trademark now, confirming the money he'd spent on **UBER4U** had been worth every cent. It was more than a plate. It was an invitation to talk, to connect, and sometimes even to flirt.

She crossed her legs slowly, deliberately, and Nick caught a glimpse of tanned, toned thigh before yanking his gaze back to the road like a priest redirecting his eyes from sin.

"We're off to Sundaze?" he asked.

"Yes, thanks, Nick." The way she said his name had a rhythm to it. Breathier this time. Like it carried extra meaning. "How long have you been doing this?"

"A few months now," he replied, keeping his eyes fixed on the traffic ahead.

"How long have you been on the road today, Nick?" she asked, sliding his name across her tongue like it was something to savour.

A pulse twitched in his temple. Something about her tone, its slow, syrupy cadence, set his instincts on edge. His gut tensed. *Be careful, mate,* it whispered.

"You're my last fare," he said.

"Lucky me," she replied, and before he could respond, she reached across and lightly traced her fingers down his forearm.

The touch was feather-light but electric, and Nick recoiled instantly, his body jerking away like he'd touched a live wire.

"Whoa," he said. "Nope. Hands to yourself."

She pouted, then leaned in closer. "You know," she purred, "I can give you a hand job for twenty, or a head job for fifty."

The offer landed hard and fast, like a slap wrapped in velvet. Nick's jaw tightened. "No thanks," he said. "I'm married."

She grinned, unbothered. "That doesn't matter. She doesn't have to know."

"Oh, yes, she does," he shot back. "I made a promise."

She cocked her head. "Okay, fine. I'll give you a head job for thirty, just for you, because you're cute." Her hand started moving again.

Nick brushed it away, firmer this time. "Look, you seem like a nice girl… but I'm not interested."

She exhaled dramatically, flipping her hair. "But I give the best head jobs," she said, like she was pitching a winning product.

"Not for me. My wife does."

The words came out sharper than he'd expected, like a final stroke of a judge's gavel. And it worked. The silence that followed was heavy but blessed.

She turned her attention to the window, arms folded, lips pursed.

Nick focused on the road, his grip tightening on the wheel. His heart was hammering, not from arousal, but from adrenaline. It hadn't been just an offer. It had been a test. A moment carved out by the universe to see if the old Nick, the weak Nick, still had a pulse. But he didn't. That man was gone.

By the time he dropped her off, she gave him a wink and blew him a kiss. He smiled, nodded once, and drove away. A quiet sense of pride filled his chest. It wasn't just that he'd said no. It was that he hadn't wanted to say yes. He hadn't even hesitated. It was a moment where temptation brushed close, offered itself on a silver platter, and he'd walked away with integrity intact and honour rising. For the first time in a long time, it felt good to be Nick Stavros.

* * *

THE REST OF Nick's week passed in a blur of passengers, conversations, and quiet revelations. Every ride carried a story, and every story reminded him of something deeper. Gratitude. Compassion. Humility. He was beginning to see life not just through his own eyes, but through the eyes of the people who passed through his car.

There was the older woman he ferried to the airport, off to visit her adult children interstate. She grumbled the entire way about how they never visited her, never called unless they needed something, and never offered to help with the cost of the flights. "I'm the one with the pension," she snorted. "But apparently, I still have to be the bank, the travel agent, and the emotional support line."

Nick listened quietly, then said gently, "Maybe it's time to stop playing the martyr." She blinked at him, startled at first, then thoughtful. He could almost hear the gears shifting in her mind. The silence that followed was thick with realisation. "You know what? You're bloody right," she said after a beat. The energy in the car lightened as she began rehearsing what she was going to say to her kids. "No more free rides. No more guilt trips. It's their turn now."

When they reached the airport, she clambered out and turned to Nick, gripping his forearm. "You're the only one who actually listens. This car of yours is better than a psychiatrist's couch. I've been paying my psych $300 an hour, and I just got what I needed for $30 with you." Then she pulled him into an unexpected bear hug, grabbed her suitcase, and marched through the sliding doors with new conviction in her step.

Another ride brought in an older couple, full of fire and opinions. By the time they'd made it halfway to their destination, they'd gone from idle chat to an impassioned debate about the state of the nation. When Nick chimed in, they lit up.

"You actually get it," the woman had said, leaning forward in her seat to keep the conversation going.

They ended up adding a stop just so the three of them could talk longer on politics, corruption, the system, and the people stuck in it. When he finally dropped them off, they were smiling and waving like old friends.

"I've never enjoyed an Uber so much," the man said, slapping the roof of the car. "Cheers, Nick. You're a legend."

But not every ride ended with laughter or insight. He'd picked up a booking for a round trip from a modest house to a local primary school. A young girl in a school uniform darted out as he pulled up, her backpack bouncing on her shoulders. "Hang on," she called over her shoulder, "Mum's coming too."

The mother stumbled out behind her, dishevelled, wide-eyed, her arms crossed tight over her chest. Nick could see the tremble in her hands, the jittery movements. Cocaine, maybe something stronger. Her eyes were red-rimmed but alert in that frantic, wired way that only drugs could produce.

On the drive to the school, the girl chatted to him about her favourite teacher. When they arrived, her mother leaned over and kissed her cheek. "Love you, baby," she said, and her daughter slid out of the car, headed for her first class.

Nick drove the mother home in silence, feeling the weight of something heavy and invisible settle between them.

When they reached the house again, she turned to him, her voice low. "I've got ways to pay for the fare… if you're interested."

Nick felt his stomach twist. Her tone wasn't seductive. It was hollow. Automatic. A transaction, not a temptation.

"No thanks," he said quietly.

She nodded, like she expected it. Slipped out of the car and disappeared behind the same door she'd come through.

Nick sat for a long moment before pulling away, his chest tight with something he couldn't quite name. Sadness, maybe. Helplessness. Anger. For the girl, who was probably packing her own school lunch that morning while her mother slept off the night before. For the mother, whose life had clearly slid so far sideways that this was how she kept the lights on. He drove in silence for a while, the hum of the engine the only sound. Then, quietly to himself, he murmured, "God, how lucky am I?"

CHAPTER SIXTEEN

The highlight of Nick's day was still the same. Coming home to Michele. After hours on the road, listening to strangers unload their secrets and longings, there was nothing he craved more than wrapping his arms around his wife and sharing the tales of his passengers. These evening debriefs had become their sacred time. Together they laughed, shook their heads, and marvelled at how strange and beautiful humanity could be. Most of all, they marvelled at each other, how far they'd come, how good it felt to be rebuilding from truth, not illusion.

There were no more conversations about betrayal, no dragging up the ghost of Joanna, or the wreckage left in the wake of lost millions. No more analysis of the friends who had ghosted them when things got rough. That chapter was closed. These days were about conscious conversation. About what they wanted to do with the time they had left. Their "third act," as Michele called it. The best act. Full of clarity, honesty, and love.

That Friday evening, as per their ritual, they sat at the bar, clinking glasses over the week that had passed. Nick sipped his scotch with a satisfied sigh. He loved these moments. These were the wins that couldn't be measured in dollars or dividends.

Michele smiled, swirling the wine in her glass. Her eyes lingered on him a moment longer than usual before she said, "Nick, I love that you've made such wonderful changes and that we're the happiest we've been in years. But please, be careful."

Nick looked up, puzzled. "What do you mean?"

She hesitated, eyes scanning the rim of her glass as if trying to find the words written there. "I don't know exactly. Just don't get caught up in believing the myth people are spinning about you. This whole 'Uber Guru' thing." She gave a soft, almost apologetic shrug. "It's sweet, and it's real to a point, but sometimes people who appear to need saving have hidden motives."

Nick blinked. "Come on. I'm just a bloke driving people around in a car, having a chat. That's hardly cult-leader material."

"I'm not saying you're doing anything wrong." She met his eyes now, firmer. "I'm just saying you've been propositioned more than once, Nick. Some of these women, hell, even some men, aren't shy. And you're alone in the car. There are no cameras, no witnesses. If anything happened, it would be your word against theirs."

A prickling discomfort climbed the back of Nick's neck. He straightened a little on the stool, half-laughing, half-defensive. "Seriously, Michele? I wonder where your mind goes sometimes."

Her gaze didn't waver. "You know how I am. I don't always know how I know things. I just know them. I'm not even sure why I said it. I've just got this feeling."

Nick leaned back, his drink suddenly a little less satisfying. He didn't like where the conversation had gone, didn't like the implication, however slight, that his integrity could be questioned. That he could end up the one painted into a corner.

Still, he knew Michele. Knew when her intuition kicked in, it was almost always right. She had that eerie sixth sense, the kind that made people turn to her for guidance without knowing why. It had saved him more than once, even when he didn't realise it at the time.

"Okay," he said finally, forcing a smile. "I'll be careful. Promise." But inside, he wasn't entirely sure what he was supposed to be careful of.

As the conversation shifted to lighter things and the last rays of sun dipped behind the horizon, Nick couldn't shake the uneasy knot in his chest. A vague sense that something was shifting again. That maybe Michele had caught the scent of a storm still hiding beyond the bend. He poured them both another drink and did his best to laugh it off. But something lingered in the air.

* * *

NICK WOKE AT his usual time—3:00 a.m. sharp. Still half-dreaming, he shuffled into the kitchen, slapped the coffee machine to life, and within minutes was lacing up his shoes, ready to hit the road. The moment he logged onto the Uber app, a ping sounded, and a job popped up, fourteen minutes away.

"Great," he muttered, stretching his back as he clicked "accept". The hum of purpose filled his chest.

Sliding behind the wheel of his beloved Greek-blue Haval, his newly installed LED windscreen UBER signs lit up through the dark like a lighthouse for lost souls. He followed the app into a quiet suburban estate, yawning into his fist, when suddenly, out of nowhere, a shirtless man came hurtling into the street, barefoot and wild-eyed, waving both arms like a runway marshal.

"Here! Here! Quick! She's about to have the baby!" he yelled.

Nick slammed on the brakes so hard his seat belt punched him in the chest. He lowered the window and shouted, "Where is she?"

The man looked over his shoulder, blinked twice, and spun back to Nick. "Oh, shit! I'll go get her!" He vanished back into the house like a meerkat on meth.

Nick blinked and shook his head. "Jesus wept." He threw the car into park and leaned out the window, shouting, "Hey! Have her waters broken?"

A muffled, "Yeah!" floated from inside.

"Then bring two towels!" Nick barked. "She's not giving birth on my bloody leather seats!"

Moments later, the chaos re-emerged. The "mother-to-be"was doubled over, gripping her partner's arm like she was trying to detach it from the socket. Her face contorted in pain. The guy clutched two mismatched towels.

Nick sprang into action. "Alright, mate. Towels on the back seat. Go. Go. Go! You" —he pointed at the woman— "you're sitting on them. Deep breaths. That's it."

The woman groaned as she clambered into the car, holding onto an overnight bag.

Nick looked at the man. "You lock the house?"

"Shit!" He bolted back up the driveway, fumbled at the door, then returned breathless.

As he jumped in, Nick threw the car into gear and peeled out of the cul-de-sac like a rally driver, flicking on his hazards. "First one?" he asked, glancing at the man in the mirror.

"Yeah!" he squeaked, face pale.

"Why aren't you driving her?" asked Nick. "It would have been quicker than waiting for me."

"I'm too bloody rattled to drive." He held up his trembling hands as evidence.

Nick shook his head, glanced at the woman, and asked, "When was your last contraction?"

The woman grunted, "Twenty minutes ago."

Nick kept his eyes on the road, ramping up the speed. "Alright. Just breathe. Deep breath in, slow breath out. Like this…" He gave a theatrical demonstration of the old Lamaze routine he'd once performed with the birth of his children.

The woman tried to follow along.

"You too!" Nick snapped at the dad. "Do it together. Breathe, puff, focus. In. Out. Like waves. Let's go!"

Both passengers began breathing like they were auditioning for a role in a childbirth documentary.

Nick sped through amber lights, calculated every corner with surgical precision, and ignored every bump as he floored it toward the hospital.

"You're doing great," he said to the mum, who was now somewhere between primal rage and spiritual transcendence. "Hold on. Just a bit longer. Don't worry. If we don't make it to the hospital, I can deliver the baby. Have done it many times before." Nick had never delivered a baby, but he'd watched his own be born, so he figured it couldn't be that hard. Anyway, his assurance seemed to settle the young woman, who gave a strained smile before returning to her breathing.

As he screeched into the hospital emergency driveway like a man possessed by the spirit of Mario Andretti, he slammed on the brakes, turned to face them, and said, "Alright. You've made it. Now go be heroes."

The man climbed out first, grabbed the bag, and then helped his partner out. "Thanks, mate," he said. "You've been a goddamn legend."

"Take your towels!" Nick called after him, pointing to the still-steaming seat where the towels remained.

The man yanked them out, and the pair hobbled into reception as hospital staff rushed toward them.

Nick exhaled, glanced at the streak of fogged-up breath on his window, and shook his head. "Well," he muttered, steering onto the empty street, "either that was a cosmic test or the universe is just taking the piss."

Maybe the next fare would be someone boring, like a tax accountant, or a guy with a quiet dog. Either way, Nick wasn't getting caught without towels again.

* * *

FARES AT THIS time of the morning usually fell into the same tired, half-lit categories—people off to early shifts in kitchens and bakeries, stragglers from nights spent on dance floors or bar stools, and women teetering between call-outs, lives held together with lashes and lip gloss. Nick had learned to predict the genre of his passengers just by glancing at the pickup pin on his map. Still, they often surprised him.

Some drunks climbed into the back like they were boarding a pirate ship, half-chanting, half-singing, demanding 80s pop hits at top volume. Others collapsed in silence, snoring through their ride as Nick silently prayed they wouldn't puke on his leather seats. There were moments of levity, like when two young women from Dublin clambered into his car, giggling uncontrollably. He couldn't tell if it was their slurred speech or their thick accents making it hard to follow, but it didn't matter. They were happy, harmless, and grateful, just like he was trying to be.

The "ladies of the night," as he now called them in his mind with an odd mix of old-school manners and modern understanding, ranged from silent and sharp-eyed to chatty and sweet. Some offered casual transactional propositions that rolled off their tongues as smoothly as the latest Taylor Swift lyrics. One woman, dressed in trackies and sneakers, confided she had a standing client at the casino, but per his request, she had to arrive in casual attire to avoid attention. She carried her sexy outfit and high heels in a plastic shopping bag. It wasn't judgment Nick felt in those moments. It was awe, confusion, and compassion; all tangled together in the same passenger seat.

Each morning felt like a procession of human frailty and resilience. He seemed to be the one steady presence in their chaotic lives. Their stories washed over him like rain, refreshing, melancholic, sometimes dangerous, but always reminding him how far he'd come. And how far he had yet to go.

* * *

By mid-morning, he found himself at a local suburban address. A woman emerged from the side path, walking toward him with such self-assurance that Nick sat up straighter behind the wheel. She was tall, mid-forties, with olive skin and jet-black hair pulled into a knot on the nape of her neck. Her stride was fluid and commanding.

"Nick?" she asked, leaning through the window.

"Yes," he replied, instantly aware of the sharp twist in his gut.

She slid into the passenger seat like smoke, all slow motion and scent; expensive perfume, undertones of spice, and something darker.

"I just need to swing by my other place. Movers are packing up." She smiled, with plump lips lined precisely in pencil.

Nick nodded, tapped the app, and drove off, trying to ignore how close her elbow was to his on the console. She wasn't flirting outright, but she was watching him. *A woman used to getting her own way,* he thought. With his eyes on the road, Nick kept to ordinary small talk, like the weather and the traffic.

"Here we are," said Nick as he pulled to the kerb.

"Thanks, Nick. I won't be a minute." She flashed him an even bigger smile.

Nick frowned. "What do you mean?"

"Check your app. I've added to this trip," she said. "Once I finish inside, you can take me back home." Another smile. "Listen, can you come inside? I just have to check on the removal company packing my things and bring out a couple of bags to take home." Without waiting for his answer, she slid out of the car and, with the same confidence, strode up the driveway to the front door.

Stunned by the request, but ever the gentleman, Nick got out of the car and followed her to the front door to help with her bags.

She edged closer to him before opening the door. "Let's play a little game, shall we?"

"What game?" he asked, now wary.

She leaned closer, conspiratorial. "There are two women inside. Let's tell them your name is Stavros and that you're my new male friend."

His spine stiffened. *Stavros. His surname. How did she…?*

Before he could ask, she was at the front door, tossing the command over her shoulder like a scarf. "Come on, Stavros."

Against his better judgment, Nick followed. Gentleman instincts, habit, or just plain shock, it didn't matter. He stepped over the threshold and into the game. The house was hollow and echoey, mostly cleared out. Two women knelt over open boxes, gently wrapping vases in tissue.

"This is Stavros," the woman announced with performative delight, wrapping her arm around his waist. "My new male friend."

Nick barely managed a nod as the packers offered bored greetings and returned to their work.

"Grab those bags for me, darling," she said, gesturing toward two designer duffels in the corner. She winked. He didn't like this game at all.

Back at the car, he stowed the bags, ready to rid himself of this passenger as quickly as possible. "Right then. Back to where I picked you up. Correct?" he asked, hands already on the wheel.

"Indeed. Thanks, Stavros," she purred his new name, continuing in the role play.

"It's Nick," he corrected, unable to keep the edge from his tone.

"Nick. Stavros. It doesn't matter, does it? It's all Greek to me." She giggled at her private joke while Nick drove a little too fast.

When they arrived, she made no move to exit alone. "Could you help me carry my bags inside, please?" she asked. "They're a little too heavy for me."

Nick eyed her with suspicion but complied and grabbed her bags from the boot. He followed her swaying form to the front door. *She may be demanding, but she sure was a looker.*

"There you go," he said, bending to drop them at the door.

"No. Come in," she said, the door already swinging open. "Just down there, please." Her long, taloned finger pointed to the end of a mirrored hallway of a designer house.

Nick obeyed with a scowl, depositing the bags where instructed. "Nice house," he said. "You and your husband have great taste."

She turned, eyes dark and glittering. "No husband. I like men too much to settle for just one. I especially like Greek men." She pressed closer. "Why don't you stay a while? I can show you a very good time."

A manicured hand slid up his arm, to his shoulder, to his neck. The scent of danger bloomed around him like a poppy field. Nick's blood ran cold. Michele's warning rang like a siren in his mind. *Be careful, Nick. If anything happens, it's your word against theirs.*

That's when everything came spinning into focus. Here he was alone in this woman's house. A woman who'd introduced him as her new male friend and was now propositioning him. He needed to get out of there fast without provoking the situation. Nick drew breath, straightened, and stared into her pooling brown eyes.

"Thank you for the offer, but I'm happily married. So, I'm going to pass."

Her hand grazed his crotch. "But, Nick, your body says yes."

Nick stepped back, eyes hard now. "You're mistaken. I'm going now."

She didn't move to stop him. "Suit yourself," she said airily. "But you're the one missing out."

Nick strode around her towards the door. Unlike Lot's wife from the Bible, he didn't look back, convinced he'd turn to stone and be doomed. He almost jogged to his car, and once inside, he sat, gripping the wheel, heart pounding.

How could I have been so stupid?

The "what-ifs" came hard and fast. What if she lied? What if she claimed he touched her, assaulted her, stole from her? What if this was a setup? He had unwittingly, though willingly, walked into it like a lamb to the slaughter.

"Fuck!" he shouted. "This is exactly what Michele warned me about."

Shame poured through him like hot tar. Anger followed: at himself, at the woman, at the thin line waiting to be crossed. It didn't matter that he'd walked away. He should never have gone in.

"You're a fuckin' idiot," he muttered. "You promised you were smarter than this."

Somewhere at the back of his mind, or was it the back seat, his grandfather's voice spoke again, low and knowing. *"It's always the same battle, Nikos. Between good and evil. And we're the prize."*

Nick stared out the windscreen, the truth of that sentence hitting him like a freight train. He'd passed the test, but it was only his word against hers. Like the story of Adam and Eve, the last time Nick had been offered the apple by a seductive woman, he had succumbed to temptation, bitten into the forbidden fruit, and nearly lost everything. Fortunately, Michele hadn't thrown him out of their Garden of Eden as God had done to Adam. She had shown him true mercy, but he knew she would only forgive once. She could only be expected to forgive once.

He needed to be more aware and realise that the battle for his integrity would be a good versus evil struggle, perhaps daily. *Well, the devil can take my business, my house, and all my material possessions, but he can't take my soul. That's the prize, and it's all mine.* Now that meaning had been restored to his life, he wasn't going to let temptation, even if it appeared wearing stilettos and a designer dress, steal that meaning away again. He'd remember this moment. He had to because this wasn't about lust or temptation anymore. It was about integrity.

"God, how am I going to tell Michele?"

"The same way you told her the truth last time," whispered his Papou. *"Just make sure you do it straight away, today."*

"Yeah. Yeah. Yeah. All right," Nick snapped out loud. "More good advice from the back seat is not what I need right now."

CHAPTER SEVENTEEN

THE JOURNEY HOME WASN'T A joyful one. Normally, the thought of wrapping his arms around Michele and sharing the day's stories would lift his heart. But today, Nick drove in silence, the radio off, the road ahead little more than a blur. His hands gripped the wheel too tightly, his shoulders tense beneath the weight of what felt like failure.

Though he hadn't crossed a line, he'd wandered too damn close. And for what? A momentary ego boost? A surge of misplaced masculinity? The shame sat like lead in his gut. Not because he'd sinned but because he'd flirted with the edge of it. Again.

You should have known better.

But this time was different. He wasn't lying. He wasn't covering his tracks. He was going to tell Michele straight away. That had to count for something. Right?

When he pulled into the driveway and stepped out, the quiet hum of evening couldn't calm the noise inside him. As he walked through the house, the smell of garlic and tomatoes wafted from the kitchen. Michele stood at the bench, slicing herbs. Her hair was tied back, her energy calm. Too calm. It almost broke him.

Nick didn't waste a second. He walked in, reached for her hands. "I had a strange situation today. Can you sit while I tell you?"

She looked up at him, her brow already furrowing with intuition. She nodded and followed him to the table, sitting without a word.

Without hesitation, he told her everything. The woman. The proposition. The moment at the door. The touch. The line he didn't cross but could have. "So, you were right," he finished, his voice low. "I should've been more aware. I never should've gone in."

There was a beat of silence. Then Michele sat back, her eyes flashing. "Or played her game in the first place." The fury came fast and hot. "Seriously, Nick, I don't get it! You're attracting these women into your life who want to take advantage of you. Stop it! Just stop it! You can't be that stupid. Surely?" She was up now, pacing. "It's like you *want* to play these stupid games. Well, I don't! I don't want to be in a marriage with a man who can't control his energy or his ego." She was out the door in an instant, slamming it behind her.

Nick remained at the table, gutted. The words clanged inside his chest like a warning bell from a sinking ship.

What the fuck am I doing?

Here he was, seventy, with no fortune, no empire, no legacy worth bragging about, playing a young man's game and nearly losing the only thing of value he had left: Michele's trust. All for a hit of admiration. A flicker of validation. A boost to his ego.

She'd warned him, and she was right. Again.

He found her in the garden, arms crossed, staring into the distance like she was weighing up everything—past, present, and possible future. He could feel the heat of her anger even before he spoke.

"I was wrong," he said. "You were right. I have no excuse. I'm sorry. I'm really sorry. Please forgive me for being so fucking stupid.

Michele didn't turn, not yet, but he saw her shoulders relax just a fraction.

"You know," she said slowly, still facing the darkening horizon, "I watched a documentary the other day. About Abraham. You know, the biblical story."

Nick blinked. "Okay…"

"Abraham lived his whole life unaware of his greater purpose. Just going through the motions. Then, at seventy, the same age as you, he got the call from God. The call to adventure. To leave everything familiar and find his true purpose. To follow something bigger than himself. And he said yes."

She turned now; her eyes locked on his. "He said yes, Nick. Abraham accepted the call and, in doing so, set off on a new path of founding the Jewish nation. He found real meaning in his life and realised his true purpose. He grew into the man he was always meant to be."

"I'm not Abraham, Michele."

"No. You're not. And I'm not saying you're supposed to father a nation. But you *are* being called. Either wake up and evolve, Nick, or die as the same man you've been most of your life, chasing shadows and sabotaging your own light. The choice is yours."

Nick stood still, her words piercing deeper than any accusation ever could.

"Wake up, Nick." She turned and walked back into the house, leaving Nick alone with the most important decision of his life.

And there, in the dusk, something shifted. He could feel it in his chest, a stirring. Not shame. Not defeat. But something else. Something sacred. He couldn't change the past, but he could change its impact and significance in his life. He could choose not to be defined by his past hurts, indiscretions, and mistakes but choose to be more, to love more, to live more fully.

He didn't need the millions of dollars promised to him. He didn't need an empire. He didn't even need redemption from anyone but himself.

Being seventy wasn't a death sentence. It was a threshold. He had walked through the valley of ego, and somehow, had made it through the other side with his soul intact. Not untouched. But intact.

Standing in the silence of his backyard, he finally understood: the battle was never with his parents, or the government, or with the people in between. The battle was within. Nick smiled through the sting of tears. He was done being his own worst enemy. This wasn't just about fidelity, or pride, or masculine bravado. It was about becoming the man Michele believed he could be. The man he believed he could be. Not a guru. Not a hero. Just a man who'd finally heard the call and chosen to answer.

* * *

From that day forward, something shifted. Nick still drove people from one point to another, but that wasn't the purpose anymore. His car became the destination. It became sanctuary, stage, confession box, and sometimes even a matchmaking booth. Passengers no longer entered merely to get somewhere. They entered to be seen, to be heard. It was as if the frequency inside the cabin vibrated a little higher, tuned in to something deeper. Something soulful.

And Nick had changed, too. He didn't force conversations or try to impress. He simply held space. He listened, asked questions when needed, and let silence do its healing work when words fell short. Somehow, everyone felt safe enough to reveal the raw, hidden parts of themselves.

That's how it was with her. She was barely more than a girl, slim, fragile, no older than twenty-one, with dark, silky hair tied in a neat plait that fell over her shoulder. When she slid into the back seat, her perfume was soft, her eyes downcast. When she spotted the string of jade beads hanging from his rear-view mirror, something shifted in her face.

"You've been to China?" she asked, tentative but curious.

Nick smiled at her in the mirror. "Twice. Once for business. The second time when my daughter got married in a small village just outside Yan Sou on the Li River."

Her face lit up. "That's where I'm from."

From that moment, the words poured out of her like a waterfall breaking free. Her name was Lin. She'd come to Australia only four months earlier on a student visa, hoping for education, opportunity, and maybe even love. But already the weight of cultural disconnection had pressed on her spirit. The boys here weren't serious, she said, not like home. The few Chinese men she'd met were either married, playing games, or interested only in partying. She spoke with equal parts yearning and quiet despair. "I'm trying to be patient," she said softly. "But it's lonely. You know? When you come from a place where family means everything, and suddenly, you are just one. Alone."

Nick's heart ached for her. Something fatherly surged up inside him, not pity, but protectiveness. When they reached her destination, the casino, where she worked part-time serving drinks, Nick didn't want to just let her go. Not without giving her something. He reached into the console for his phone and turned to her. "Here. Put your name and number in here."

She hesitated; brows knitted. "Why?"

"In case I find someone for you," he said, grinning. "You never know. My car's full of people. Could be someone looking for you right now."

A soft smile spread across her face, as if the idea alone rekindled some small flame of hope. She keyed in her number carefully, thanked him with a slight bow, and stepped out.

Nick hadn't even put the car in drive when his app pinged again. A new fare. Same location.

Casino pick-up.

Nick chuckled under his breath. "Well, that didn't take long."

Less than a minute later, a young man slid into the passenger seat beside him. Trim, well-groomed, early twenties. Nick's eyes flicked to the mirror out of habit. He was Chinese too.

As Nick pulled out, he felt a familiar tickle at the back of his mind. The bell again. That strange tingle told him to pay attention. "How's your day?" Nick asked casually.

The young man sighed. "Tiring. Girls these days don't want anything serious. I don't know, man. I just want something real."

Nick turned slightly, raising an eyebrow. "You single?"

The young man laughed. "Obviously. Or I wouldn't be talking like this."

Nick grinned and couldn't help himself. "Well, you might think I'm crazy, but I just dropped off a young woman ten minutes ago who said the exact same thing. Pretty girl. From Yan Sou. Looking for Mr. Right."

The man leaned forward. "Seriously?"

Nick reached for his phone at a red light. "What's your name?"

"Jun."

"Okay, Jun. I'm going to play matchmaker for the first time in my Uber career."

Nick pulled over and texted Lin a simple message:

"Met someone. Your male twin. Would you like me to connect you?"

Her reply was instant:

"Yes. Please. Thank you."

He passed on the contact, smiling like a matchmaker who'd just witnessed the stars align.

But it wasn't just about romance. It was about human connection. It was about two lonely hearts being nudged into orbit around each other by a man who'd once almost lost everything, and now, through the simplest of gestures, was helping others find their way home.

Nick didn't expect anything more to come of it. But a week later, Lin sent him a message:

"Thank you, Nick. We had coffee. Then dinner. We're seeing where it goes. But I think there may be a future for us together."

Nick stared at the text for a long time. It was a quiet moment. Something inside Nick lit up. Not pride. Not ego. Purpose. Perhaps his purpose was to bring people together and not just drive them around.

The lonely women still paraded in and out of his car, but now, Nick saw them differently. They weren't temptresses or trouble; they were tired. Tired of giving more than they got. Tired of hoping and hurting and explaining themselves to people who didn't listen. Their pain wasn't dramatic, just worn in like a second skin. Some were quiet, drifting in and out of the back seat like ghosts. Others were talkative, filling the car with stories of ex-husbands, failed dates, friends who'd disappeared when life got hard. Betrayals that came without daggers, but with silence.

Nick listened. Not with judgment, but with the kind of presence that only comes from someone who's been on both sides of betrayal, perpetrator and victim. And always their stories brought him back to Michele.

Every time a woman said, "I caught him cheating and he blamed me," or "He ghosted me after five years," or "I thought we were building something together," Nick felt a quiet throb of gratitude. Not guilt anymore, not shame, but a grounded, reverent kind of thanks. Michele had forgiven him. She'd taken the risk to trust him again. That was no small thing. Every woman who stepped into his car reminded him not to take that gift for granted. Forgiveness, he realised, wasn't a one-time event. It was a daily act of love. One he had to earn over and over.

He was also beginning to see that betrayal wasn't rare. It was universal. People betrayed one another all the time, for power, for ego, out of fear, out of selfishness. Partners, parents, siblings, bosses. No one was exempt, which meant that forgiveness, too, was always possible, if not now, then maybe someday.

He was slowly working on forgiving his own family. His brother. Even, maybe, his father. It wasn't easy. Some days, he woke up feeling open, ready to let go. Other days, he gripped the past like a steering wheel on a slippery road. As

Michele reminded him, that was the work. Evolving wasn't some big, dramatic overhaul. It was a hundred small choices made moment by moment.

Still, not every ride was heavy with sorrow. Many came with moments of levity.

"Where can I find someone like you?" women would ask, eyes hopeful.

"Do you have a brother who's single? A cousin? A clone?"

Nick would chuckle, shake his head. "Afraid not. I'm a limited edition."

It always earned a laugh, sometimes a playful sigh. Occasionally, someone would leave a lipstick print on his cheek at the "Kiss and Ride" drop-off zone, like a thank-you stamp for listening. He allowed those sweet, harmless gestures because he understood where they came from. Not flirtation. Just a hunger to be seen. To feel a moment of connection with someone who wasn't trying to fix or seduce or manipulate.

If a five-minute ride could do that for someone, could make them feel heard and human again, then who was he to refuse?

He started noticing that his biggest tips came from these women. Not the flashy ones or the high-flyers, but the lonely ones. The grateful ones. Women who were thrilled to have been treated like a person, not a problem. Women hungry for kindness, starved for a little affection that didn't come with a bill or an asterisk.

One woman in her sixties, elegant, with silver hair and deep-set eyes, had reached over and touched his arm before stepping out.

"You give me hope that decent men still exist," she'd said, voice trembling.

Nick sat there a long time after she left, watching people blur past the windows. He wasn't perfect. God knows, he'd failed hard and often. But if even one woman walked away from his car feeling more hopeful about love, about men, about life, then maybe, just maybe, he was becoming the man Michele believed he could be.

Maybe that was the point of all this. Not to be perfect. But to keep showing up with one's heart intact, eyes open, and hands steady on the wheel.

CHAPTER EIGHTEEN

Michele sat cross-legged on her meditation stool in the centre of her stone circle, wrapped in a shawl of woven wool, its fringe brushing the frost-kissed grass. Even through her thick socks, the morning chill clung to her skin, whispering the first notes of winter's song. The sun had long breached the horizon, but its warmth was still timid, filtering softly through the mist like a promise not yet spoken.

Normally, she would have returned inside by now, into the familiar rhythms of the kitchen, the kettle's whistle, the clink of mugs. Today, she lingered. Something in the air, perhaps the stillness, perhaps the slow tilt of light, invited her to stay just a little longer with her thoughts.

It had been over nine months since Nick detonated the truth of his betrayal and sent a fault line through the bedrock of their marriage. Nine months. A human life could begin and be born in that span. In a way, something had been born. Not something new exactly, but something reformed. Refined. Tempered in fire.

It had taken her three of those months just to forgive herself, for her rage, for her sorrow, for the part of her that had doubted her own worth. Then, a little more time to forgive him. Not just in words, but in the quiet, everyday grace of letting love return. Now, after six months of watching Nick prove himself, not just through apologies, but through effort and humility, she felt something settle in her heart. A softness. A quiet pride.

They had traversed this terrain together. Rocky, uneven, often painful, but they hadn't taken the easy route of burying it beneath platitudes or pretending everything was fine, like many of their friends had suggested. No. They had stood in the debris, hand in hand, and chosen to rebuild. Slowly. Truthfully. Gently.

That is why it had worked. That's why they were stronger now, not in spite of what had happened, but because of it. No resolution was ever realised without self-forgiveness. She had learned, again and again, that forgiveness was not a single decision but a series of choices, each one opening the door just a little wider to love.

She breathed in the crisp air, her eyes closed. The scent of damp earth, eucalyptus, and something floral caught in the breeze. She smiled.

Nick was changing. Not dramatically. Not loudly. But in small, tangible ways. Consistent ways. He had made good on his promises. Waking before dawn, driving all day, coming home with stories and laughter and the kind of quiet joy she hadn't seen in him in years. It wasn't the money. God knew the Uber driving barely covered the bills, but it was the meaning that mattered. He was finally doing something with heart.

As she knew how hard it was for him. At seventy, to be driving strangers around for hours, for less than minimum wage, wasn't glamorous. But it was honest. It was his penance and his path. His road back to the light, and that made it sacred.

She'd walked a similar road in her younger years when she'd had to rebuild herself from the inside out. She knew the loneliness of that inner work, the invisible labour of it. She knew the reward was rarely gold or glory, but something more precious: *Peace. Self-respect. Resonance.*

All Nick had to do now was keep reaching for that higher frequency, not perfection, not power, just peace. To remember that being right wasn't nearly as important as feeling good. That joy didn't arrive at a destination; it lived in the journey. It always had.

She opened her eyes and looked toward the house. On Sundays, Nick would join her outside, wrapped in his old hoodie, bringing her a second cup of coffee. But not today. By now, he'd have been on the road for at least three hours, finding his own joy in the journey.

Last year, his seventieth birthday had come and gone without fanfare. He'd refused to celebrate it, drowning instead in guilt and whiskey and curses for his dead parents. That day had felt like a funeral for his youth, for his unfulfilled dreams. But this year, things were going to be different. Michele had already planned a quiet dinner with the kids.

"A belated seventieth," she'd told them. They understood. They'd seen the shift in their father, too. They would come and celebrate.

A sudden shaft of sunlight broke through, golden and warm on her face. Michele tilted her chin upward, eyes closed once more, letting it soak into her skin.

A sign, she thought, *of brighter years ahead.*

She didn't know what the future held. But she knew they were walking toward it, side by side. Awake. Humble. Hopeful.

* * *

"You are not going to believe what happened in the car today," Nick called as he burst into the kitchen like a kid fresh off a roller coaster.

Michele arched an eyebrow. "Is it good or bad?"

"It's not bad. Just… unbelievable!" His eyes gleamed. "Come on, grab a drink. I need props for this story."

Intrigued, Michele followed him out to the summer house, where he was already pouring two glasses of scotch with the kind of flourish usually reserved for stage magicians.

"Right," he said, handing her a glass. He lit a cigarette, took a dramatic drag, and exhaled slowly. "Buckle up. This is a cracker."

"Do I need to sit down?" Michele asked, moving to the lounge.

"Definitely." A beat. "I pick up this young English couple from the hotel. Mid-twenties, maybe. He's all polite and shy, and she's the mouthpiece. Talkative, animated, full of beans. Pretty girl. Big smile. Cheeky glint in her eye. We're cruising along, and she's leaning forward between the seats, talking about Aussie nightlife, their holiday, all the usual stuff. Then out of nowhere, she goes, 'You seem pretty broad-minded. Are you?'"

Michele's eyes narrowed in amusement. "And you said?"

"I said yes. I mean. I had no idea what was coming next, but I figured it wasn't going to be about sightseeing." Nick took another swig. "Then she says, and I quote… 'Our fantasy is for me to give my boyfriend a blowjob in the backseat of a car while someone drives. Would you mind?'"

Michele blinked. "What?!"

"I know!" Nick slapped his thigh and laughed. "I'm sitting there, trying not to choke on my own tongue. So, I said, real calm, 'I don't care what you do as long as you don't get spoof on the seats.'"

Michele exploded in laughter. "Oh, my God, Nick!"

"I was serious!" he said, grinning. "This is a brand-new car. Leather seats. Not cleaning DNA off them for anyone, no matter how polite they are."

"And then what did she say?"

"She goes, 'Don't worry, I always swallow. Never miss a drop.' Then pulls out a packet of tissues like it's a formal dinner and she's brought the serviettes."

Michele had tears in her eyes now. "You let them go through with it?"

"Look, they were in love, or at least very enthusiastic. Honestly, it reminded me of us, back in the day. Sneaking off, doing outrageous stuff for the thrill of it." Nick smiled fondly. "So, I said, 'Knock yourselves out.'"

Michele shook her head in disbelief, beaming. "You're telling me that while you were driving through the city, that girl was…"

Nick raised his glass. "Neck-deep in fulfilling her bucket list."

"Oh, my God," Michele said again, half laughing, half wheezing. "What happened when they finished?"

"She popped back up like a Cheshire cat, wiped her mouth, grinned at me in the rear-view mirror, and said, 'See? Not a drop.' Proud as punch."

"And him?"

"He zipped up, leaned forward, and said, 'Cheers, man. You're a legend.'"

Michele doubled over. "Please tell me they tipped."

"Twenty bucks!" Nick held up two fingers like he was reporting a poker win. "A blowie and a bonus. Best ride ever, I reckon."

"They'll be dining out on that story for the rest of their lives," Michele said, still cackling. "The Uber of dreams. Five stars and a happy ending."

Nick winked. "Not for me, sadly."

"Oh, poor you," she teased, nudging him. "So selfless."

They sat in the fading light, their laughter settling into warmth. It was these moments, this ease, this shared wickedness that made Nick feel most like himself. That he and Michele could laugh at life, rather than be crushed by it.

"Funny, isn't it?" said Nick. "How we've ended up right here. After everything. Laughing about blowjobs and back seats like we're twenty-five again."

Michele smiled, her hand sliding over his. "We've earned it. Every laugh. Every wrinkle. Every mad, delicious moment."

Nick kissed the top of her hand and raised his glass. "To being broad-minded."

"To leather seats and no DNA," she toasted. Michele leaned in, her eyes twinkling with mischief. "You know, we could go inside and relive some of our own naughty moments. For old times' sake."

Nick chuckled, his grin widening. "Absolutely."

She stood, extending her hand to him. "Come on, my Uber Guru. Let's make some new memories to laugh about."

And under the twilight sky, with the sounds of the world softening around them, they adjourned to the bedroom, a couple of aging rebels, still finding joy in the ride.

* * *

As weeks turned into months, Nick discovered a new rhythm to his days. The car became a place where stories were shared, laughter echoed, and healing began. Each morning, he donned one of his brightly coloured floral shirts, a nod to his vibrant heritage and a symbol of his renewed zest for life.

Reflecting on his journey, Nick often recalled his psychologist's explanation of the five stages of grief: denial, anger, bargaining, depression, and acceptance. He recognized each phase in his own transformation. Denial had cloaked his early justifications; anger had flared at his own missteps; bargaining had come with desperate promises; depression had settled in during the darkest nights. But now, acceptance wrapped around him like a warm embrace. Though he still grappled with shame for his actions, he understood that while he couldn't change the past, he could shape the future.

Each afternoon, returning home became a cherished ritual. He'd park his car, the blue paint gleaming in the sunlight, and take a moment to appreciate the life he'd rebuilt. Cleaning the car wasn't just maintenance, it was a meditation, a way to honour the journeys shared within its walls.

Joining Michele in the summer house for a pre-dinner drink, they'd share stories of their day, laughter bubbling between sips. The pain of the past had softened, replaced by a deeper connection forged through honesty, resilience, and the restoration of trust.

Life, with all its twists and turns, felt good again. Not because it was perfect, but because they had chosen to embrace the journey together, finding joy in each moment and love in every shared glance.

CHAPTER NINETEEN

"O KAY, WHAT'S THE STORY?"
It had become a kind of unofficial catchphrase among Nick's passengers. An opening line that cracked open the door to curiosity, an invitation to tell, or to be told.

Nick had heard it dozens of times by now, always with a bemused expression and a glance around his car. His standard reply, equal parts cheeky and sincere, was: "What do you mean?"

And the answers never varied by much. "There must be more to you than being a rideshare driver." Or, "You don't look like the Uber type." Or even, "Why's this car so clean and smells good? What's the aftershave you're wearing?"

Nick would simply smile, answer them politely, and let them talk. Because before long, comments became conversation. Conversation became connection. And connection… that was the real fare. Each five-star rating he earned wasn't because of the model of the car or the polish of the leather seats (though he did keep them damn near spotless). It was because Nick saw his passengers not just as fares, but as fellow humans in all their chaos, pain, hope, humour, and heartbreak. Like him, they were all just trying to get somewhere. Find something. Maybe even someone. They wanted, like he did, to feel the joy in their journey.

"Nick?" a man asked now, opening the passenger door.

"That's me."

The man held the door open for a woman and a curly-haired little girl, maybe four years old, who clambered eagerly into the back seat. Once they were settled, he slipped into the front passenger seat with a weary sigh.

As Nick eased into traffic, the man wasted no time. "We're on holiday from Melbourne," he began, his voice a mixture of exhaustion and release, as though finally being able to say it out loud might make it more bearable. "But it's not really a holiday. We're here to look for a way out."

Nick glanced sideways, sensing the freight train of frustration about to arrive.

"Victoria is lost," the man continued. "The city is a ghost town. Businesses have been gutted. Immigrants are roaming the streets with machetes. The government has destroyed the state, our home, and our children's futures. We're done."

"It's a bloody disgrace," his wife added from the back, the words heavy with disappointment. Her voice carried the sadness of someone who once loved where she lived but was now betrayed by it.

Nick met her eyes in the rear-view mirror. She looked tired and sad.

"We've been looking at houses all week," the man added. "Seen fifteen. Still not sure. But we're not going back."

Nick nodded, understanding the story of disillusionment and grief of leaving a life once loved, and the quiet search for somewhere safer to rebuild.

Before he could reply, the small voice of the child in the back seat piped up, bright with innocence. "Daddy," she asked, "why are there so many people for sale?"

Nick glanced up, puzzled. The little girl was pointing at the dozens of corflute signs with the smiling faces of polished political candidates staked along the grassy verge like a real estate buffet.

Her parents blinked, confused at first. Then the misunderstanding dawned, and they laughed.

"Oh, sweetheart," the mother said, reaching for her daughter's hand. "Those aren't 'For Sale' signs. They're election signs. Those are people asking us to vote for them."

The girl scrunched her nose. "Well, they look for sale."

Nick snorted. "To be fair, most of them *are*. Just depends on who's buying."

The mother burst out laughing, while the father gave Nick a double tap on the shoulder. "Bang on, mate. Couldn't have said it better."

As the car filled with easy chuckles, Nick felt that familiar lightness begin to bubble up again. That strange, sacred blend of absurdity and truth. Leave it to a child to name what adults dance around: so much of life did look like a giant "For Sale" sign.

And yet there were still pockets of goodness. These passengers, for example, were choosing courage over comfort. Starting again. He understood that feeling more than he ever thought he would.

As they drove on, the political signs blurred past in quick succession, each smile faker than the last. But the voices and the energy in the car felt real. Nick smiled to himself. It was all about perception, wasn't it? Same sign, different eyes. Same road, different story. Same man… but he was no longer the same.

Because the longer he drove, the more he realised something essential: it wasn't about what life took from you, or how many times you'd been knocked down, or betrayed, or left behind. It was about how many times you said yes to joy anyway. Said yes to connection. Yes to the ride.

Every trip was a new lesson, a fresh reminder that the joy wasn't just in the destination, it was in the becoming. In the silly misinterpretations. In the overheard secrets. In the broken hearts and hopeful new beginnings. In humanity.

And as Nick turned off the main road, his eyes crinkled with something close to awe. The world might be a mess. People might be for sale. But as long as he could still laugh with strangers and find light in the cracks, he'd keep driving. Keep listening. Keep showing up. Because maybe that's what it meant to be human: to stay on the road, to keep your eyes open, and, most of all, to find joy in the ride.

* * *

WITH THE SUN slowly arcing across the sky, Nick pulled the Haval to the kerb where a distinguished-looking man in a dark suit leaned lightly on a polished wooden walking stick. His shoes were shined, his grey hair neatly combed, and his upright posture hinted at a man who still valued dignity, even if his body now required assistance.

"Are you Nick?" called the gentleman, ducking his head toward the window.

"Yes. That's me," Nick replied, checking the app. "Mr. Lockhart?"

The older man nodded.

"Do you need a hand?"

"No. I'm fine," he said, with the sort of gracious defiance Nick recognised all too well in aging men, an insistence on independence, even when it came at the cost of comfort. Mr. Lockhart wrestled with the cane and manoeuvred himself into the front passenger seat, his movements slow but deliberate.

"Off to the hospital, right?" Nick confirmed, tapping the app to start the journey.

"Yes, thank you," the man replied, settling back into the seat with a weary sigh. He had soft blue eyes, alert but kind, and a stillness about him that was calming. "So, Nick," he said after a beat, "have you been driving long?"

Nick smiled. "Not forever. Let's just say I took the scenic route to get here."

He gave Mr. Lockhart a short version of his life story, leaving out the more salacious details, but before he could finish, the gentleman held up a hand.

"I'm eighty-seven years old," he said, "and I've come to understand that life only works if you live by four simple rules."

Nick raised an eyebrow. "Just four? That's either very wise or very optimistic."

Mr. Lockhart chuckled. "Probably both. But if you remember nothing else, remember these."

He ticked them off slowly, one by one, his voice steady and sure.

"First, build financial equity. Spend less than you earn, every single day."

Nick nodded. "Wish I'd started that one a few decades ago."

"Second, invest in people. Especially your family. Help them succeed and you'll build generational equity, something far more valuable than money."

A quiet pang struck Nick in the chest. He thought of his kids. The will. The bitterness. He gave a small, regretful nod.

"I don't think I've done enough of that," he said quietly. "My Papou tried, but I guess I didn't really get it. Until now."

Mr. Lockhart placed a comforting hand on his arm. "It's not too late. You're still young."

Nick grinned. "Well, not that much younger than you."

"Third," Mr. Lockhart went on, "become self-educated. Never take anyone's opinion as gospel. Go find the truth for yourself."

"Oh, I'm on board with that one," Nick said. "I've read more in the past two years than I ever did in school. Truth's out there, just not always where you think it is."

"And finally," said Mr. Lockhart, his voice softening, "place love, loyalty, and legacy before anything else. That's how you live a good life."

Nick's hand froze on the steering wheel. Those weren't just words. They were the exact words his Papou had spoken to him, inside Nick's mind, months ago. It had changed the direction of his life.

Nick turned toward his passenger, his voice tight. "Who are you?"

Mr. Lockhart smiled gently. "Just a man going to the hospital to visit his wife."

There was something in the way he said it, casual, deflective, almost playful, but Nick didn't push.

"How is she?"

"She's been in there for four days. They won't tell me anything." He lifted a plastic container from inside a grocery bag. "I bring her food every day. The hospital stuff isn't fit for anyone, let alone someone who's ill."

"What do you mean they won't tell you?" Nick asked, a flare of anger lighting inside him.

"They treat me like I'm invisible. An old fool. After forty years as a university lecturer, I've become someone to be spoken down to or not at all."

Nick looked over and saw the faint glint of tears in Mr. Lockhart's pale eyes.

"Don't you have family here?"

"My daughter's interstate. She means well. She books my Ubers. But she can't get time off to come."

Nick wanted to say something, but held back the judgment. Life was messy. Still, the idea of this man, dignified and still so lucid, being dismissed so easily hit a nerve.

As the hospital approached, a sudden decision gripped him. "Would you like me to come in and help get some answers?"

The old man looked at him, surprised. "Would you really?"

Nick nodded. "Yeah. No worries. I'll park and switch the app off." He turned into the car park, snagged a ticket, and parked in the shade. Hopping out, he rushed around to open the door and offer his hand. Mr. Lockhart accepted it with a grateful smile.

"You know, Nick… there are very few people with your compassion. It's rare. Hold onto it."

They made their way into the hospital and up to the third floor. At Room 314, Mr. Lockhart paused at the door, smoothed his jacket, and stepped inside. "Mary, love, I'm here."

A small woman in the bed lifted her head. Despite her pallor, her eyes brightened at the sound of his voice. "Henry," she whispered. "You're early today."

"I brought you chicken with lemon and rosemary," he said, holding up the bag with boyish pride.

"And who is this handsome man?"

"This is Nick," Henry said. "My Uber driver and now my advocate."

Mary smiled. "Well, thank you, Nick. I can see why Henry took a liking to you."

A nurse entered just then. "Excuse me, are you family?"

Nick stood tall. "No. I'm here as a friend. But Mr. Lockhart hasn't received any updates on his wife's condition in four days. We'd like to speak with the doctor now, please." Something in Nick's tone brooked no argument.

Within minutes, a young doctor arrived, holding a clipboard. "I'm sorry for the delay. We've been running tests," he began. "Unfortunately, the scans show the cancer has returned and progressed significantly. It's metastasised. I'm sorry, Mary, but we're going to have to move you to palliative care."

The silence that followed was thick with reverence, not shock.

Mary reached out and took Henry's hand. "Well," she said softly, "we had a good run, didn't we?"

"The best," he replied, gently brushing her cheek.

Nick felt his chest cave in slightly. He wasn't supposed to be here. But somehow, he was. Bearing witness and learning something he hadn't understood until right this second.

Mary looked up at him again, her voice faint but firm. "Don't waste time, Nick. Love your wife. Treasure your family. Nothing else matters."

Henry nodded. "All the money in the world can't buy what we built together."

Nick swallowed hard. "Thank you. Both of you."

They smiled. Two old souls. Facing the end with grace.

As he left the room, Nick paused at the doorway, one last look over his shoulder. The image of their intertwined hands stayed with him long after he returned to the car. He sat in the Haval, hands on the wheel, but he didn't start the engine. He tried to swallow the lump in his throat, but it refused to budge.

All this time, he thought. *I've been chasing money, power, recognition, thinking those things made me a man. Thinking they made me free.*

But love… loyalty… legacy. That was the real wealth. That was the freedom. Not in his bank account. But in his heart. He was already rich. And now it was time to share it.

CHAPTER TWENTY

"HAPPY BIRTHDAY TO YOU…"
The final note lingered in the warm air like a prayer, held a beat longer by a chorus of familiar voices before erupting into applause, laughter, and cheers. The scent of grilled lamb and garlic filled the evening breeze, blending with the distant crash of waves from the nearby bay. Candlelight flickered across faces that held decades of memory, forgiveness, and love.

Nick stood at the head of the table, blinking back the emotion in his eyes as he gazed at the people gathered around him, his children, their partners, and his grandchildren, all of them radiant with life. His tribe. His legacy. The reflection of every hard choice and every humble truth he'd finally embraced.

They had come together at *Mykonos*, his favourite Greek restaurant, a brilliant white-and-blue haven perched above the shoreline, its painted shutters and mosaic-tiled terrace a loving homage to his roots. This wasn't just a birthday dinner. It was a quiet triumph, a culmination. A celebration not of a number, but of a man reborn.

He bent over the candlelit cake, the flickering flames dancing in the breeze, and drew in a steady breath. Then, with the calm of a man who finally knew who he was, he exhaled. Cheers rang out again.

He leaned close to Michele and pressed a kiss to her cheek, his lips lingering there longer than necessary, as if to anchor himself in the reality of this joy. "This is wonderful, darling," he whispered, his voice thick with gratitude. "Thank you for organising this. It means more than you know."

She turned to him, her eyes soft and shining. "Thank you, Nick, for becoming the man I fell in love with… and more. I'm so proud of you."

He held her gaze. "No, thank you. None of this would have happened without your love. Your forgiveness saved me. I love you more than I'll ever be able to say."

Before she could reply, a small, determined hand tugged at his wrist. "Come on, Papou. Come with us!" said young Nicholas, recently turned seven, his brown eyes wide with mischief and joy.

Nick laughed and allowed himself to be pulled away. The children swarmed him, their excited voices overlapping as they led him out onto the terrace balcony. The sea stretched before them in a soft blue hush, dotted with boats rocking gently in the twilight. This was the inheritance worth fighting for.

"So, what's it like to be old, Papou?" asked Ari, the eldest, who stood with the straight-backed authority of his ten years.

Nick chuckled. "Seventy-one isn't old, Ari. In fact, a wise man told me I was young." He gave them a wink and drew them in close. Their faces upturned with curiosity. "So that means," he continued, "we have plenty of time to get to know each other better and for me to tell you stories about life."

A collective groan rose from the group. "We just want to play, Papou!"

He laughed from deep in his chest, the kind of laughter that only comes from a soul at peace. "We'll do plenty of that too," he promised. "But why don't we take a little walk? I'll tell you about the four most important rules a wise man once shared with me. And maybe," he added with a conspiratorial smile, "we'll grab an ice cream along the way."

Cheers erupted, and small hands reached for his, wrapping around his fingers and pulling him forward. As they wandered toward the beach path, the golden light of dusk stretched their shadows long behind them. Nick felt a surge of emotion rise in his chest, so full it almost hurt.

From somewhere in the recesses of his memory or perhaps from somewhere else entirely, his Papou's voice echoed, as clear as the sky above them. *"To find one's purpose is the greatest quest any man can make. I am proud of you, Nikos. You placed love, loyalty, and legacy before all else. And now, life's greatest rewards are yours."*

Nick slowed his steps and glanced back toward the restaurant. Through the wide, open doors, he spotted Michele still at the table, watching him with a knowing smile. She blew him a kiss, and in that moment, something soft but seismic shifted in him.

He had spent so many years measuring his worth against things that never really mattered. Money. Success. Praise. Freedom, he once believed, came from having more. But standing here, hand-in-hand with the future, looking back at the woman who had helped him reclaim his true self, he finally understood the truth:

Freedom was love. Wealth was family. And purpose was found in showing up for those who needed him. His heart brimmed with joy. He was no longer a man chasing something. He was a man who had arrived. As the sea breeze tousled his hair and the children skipped ahead into the soft light of evening, Nick followed, steady and sure.

Just a man.

A Papou.

A husband.

A heart cracked open by life and filled to overflowing.

Home.

EPILOGUE

Nick and Michele's story does not end here. In truth, it never ends. Their lives, like yours, are ever evolving, pulsing with growth, echoing with the rhythms of human longing and divine possibility. What you've witnessed is not a finish line, but the crossing of a sacred threshold: from survival to significance, from brokenness to becoming, from disconnection to wholeness.

Yes, there were still difficult days. Even after his transformation, Nick sometimes found himself drifting back into the gravity of old disappointments. Wounds from childhood, betrayals long buried, regrets tied like knots in his chest; these resurfaced from time to time in sarcastic comments and dark moods. Growth, after all, is not a straight line, but a spiral. He took responsibility and circled back, not to fall but to rise a little higher each time. And rise he did.

Michele, though radiant in grace, wrestled too. There were moments when the old shadows returned, whispers of unworthiness, echoes of the betrayal that once shattered her trust. But even in those quiet storms of the heart, she stood in the stillness and chose to love again. Not blindly, not naively, but bravely. She understood something that many never grasp. Forgiveness is not forgetting; it is remembering with compassion instead of pain.

Together, they kept choosing each other. Kept choosing joy. Kept choosing to laugh, even when life offered little reason to do so. They learned that joy isn't the absence of difficulty but the alchemy of presence—that humour, humility, and holding hands are sometimes the most powerful forms of healing. And so, their journey continued, not on a pedestal, but on the rich and messy earth of real human experience.

When the world around them began to shift once more with economies faltering, systems crumbling, certainties vanishing, they felt a deeper stirring. The call to an unexpected adventure. It came not as a thunderous command from the heavens, but a quiet pull in the chest. An inner nudge that said: *It's time. Go north. Find peace near the sea.*

And they answered my call and dared to follow.

Despite the resistance of habit and the comfort of the familiar, they packed up their home, their memories, their regrets, and their dreams and relocated to a gentler place. A place where the ocean's breath whispered a new rhythm into their days. There, they found a quieter kind of wealth: space to breathe, sunrises without rush, new friendships without pretence.

Nick continued to drive, not because he had to, but because he wanted to. Every passenger was still a mirror, every journey a sermon. His rides became softer, slower, and more spacious. Sometimes he'd say little. Sometimes he'd listen deeply. But always, he held his passengers in a sacred field of respect and respite. His car remained what it had become, a sanctuary on wheels.

Then, almost like a final bow from the universe, the shares he had long held finally bore fruit. Not in the wild riches he once chased, but in a steady abundance that came without struggle. It was never about the money. It was always about the man he needed to become before the manifestation.

Now, life flows for Nick and Michele in a steady, sacred hum. A dance of morning walks, salty breezes, grandchildren's giggles, and nights under the stars. They are not perfect. They do not seek to be. They simply live awake with their hearts unarmoured and eyes open to wonder, anchored to an inner consciousness.

They know now that the only constant in life is change. Change is not meant to punish, but to polish. Not to test, but to teach. Each challenge is not a judgement, but an invitation: *Will you rise again? Will you trust? Will you dare to be more and say yes to joy?*

This was never just their story. It's your story too.

Because you, dear reader, have also been betrayed. You have doubted your worth. You have walked through shadows and questioned the point of it all. Yet, you are still here. Still becoming. Still being invited to begin again.

Like Nick, you may have thought your value was measured in wealth or achievement. But the treasure has always lived in your heart, in your capacity to forgive, to start anew, to love anyway. The real freedom you seek isn't out there. It lives inside your curiosity and willingness to show up for your own life, fully and freely, and let the chips fall where they may.

So, if today feels heavy, if the road behind you is littered with mistakes or regrets, let this story remind you: *You are not your past. You are your promise.*

You, too, can rise. You, too, can choose love over pride, truth over comfort, joy over cynicism. And when you do… when you say yes to the call, again and again and again, you will find that life does not punish the broken. It crowns them.

Trust the detour.

Employ more joy.

Forgive for no other reason than you deserve it.

Share love in all its expressions.

And keep putting one foot in front of the other, no matter how difficult it may seem.

For when you do, when you dare to be more than before, you never walk alone.

I am the silence between your thoughts.

I am the breath that steadies your fear.

I am the light that guides your way into the unknown.

I am your every act of courage, your every gesture of gratitude.

I am (with) you always.

THE END

AFTERWORD BY DIANE

AN INNER THOUGHT FROM MICHELE, one of the main characters in *The Reluctant Uber Guru*:

"Deep inside Nick, there was a light that had once illuminated her world. A soul that had touched hers so profoundly, so unmistakably, that even now, she could feel it flickering through the darkness. It was faint, shadowed by pain and mistakes. But it was still there."

Michele's inner strength gave her the determination to strive for what she once took for granted. There would be many trials, but she wouldn't give Nick up without a fight. Why?

Learn the truth about Michele and Nick's love story from the beginning, in *Tempt Me*:

One woman… Two men… Threesomes change everything

When Michele Johnston, a forty-two-year-old ex-dancer from the Moulin Rouge, gets divorced, she leaps into her new world of singledom with unbridled passion.

Aided and abetted by three vivacious girlfriends, Michele embarks on her steamy, erotic adventures, but gets more than she expects when mysterious yacht captain Mark Miller unleashes her wanton desires.

Further complicating matters, debonair Greek businessman Nick Stavros arrives on the scene and falls madly in love with her, promising the happy-ever-after ending. But will she give up her newfound freedom? Will she choose one man over the other? Or can she continue loving them both?

Tempt Me is the first stand-alone Contemporary Erotic Romance in Diane Demetre's genre-busting series, Steamy Secrets. If you love strong heroes, hot sex, and feisty heroines, don't miss this page-turning love story with a twist.

Reader Advisory: A Contemporary Erotic Romance containing a sexually empowered heroine and willing men to fulfil her desires. Casual sex scenes with recreational drug use.

Find out more at dianedemetre.com

KEYNOTE SPEAKER

Diane Demetre is an award-winning business leader, author, and former professional entertainer turned high-impact keynote speaker. With over 40 years' experience across entrepreneurship, education, and entertainment, she's been named *Most Empowering Leadership & Mindset Speaker* in 2024 & 2025 and has been the recipient of the *International Women's Day Leadership Award.* These days, she helps leaders and teams *activate their state*—elevating energy, boosting engagement, and sparking real results… with a little razzle-dazzle along the way.

Find out more at dianedemetre.com

AWARD-WINNING AUTHOR

"Dare to dream bigger than ever before, dare to forge your own path, no matter how hard the challenges. But most of all, dare to be you and let the chips fall where they may. We are all warrior women with gossamer wings…It's time to soar!"

—Diane Demetre

Winner of the 2019 SBAA International Women's Day Leader Award for Leadership in the Entertainment, Creative Arts, and/or Media Industry.

Diane was nominated as a finalist in the ARRA Awards 2018 for Favourite Romantic Suspense, for her novel *Retribution*.

In 2017, Diane won the Romance Writers of Australia Emerald Pro Award for Best Unpublished Romance Manuscript, for her novel *Retribution*.

ALSO, BY DIANE DEMETRE

NON-FICTION

Master Mindset
Dare

FICTION

A Diana Daniels Mystery series:
Evil on the High Seas
Killer in the Outback

Steamy Secrets series:
Tempt Me
Teach Me
Take Me

Standalone Fiction:
Retribution
Island of Secrets

DIANE DEMETRE